CW00677638

Thomas Wir.

Curate V3

George MacDonald

Alpha Editions

This edition published in 2023

ISBN : 9789357946339

Design and Setting By
Alpha Editions
www.alphaedis.com
Email - info@alphaedis.com

As per information held with us this book is in Public Domain.
This book is a reproduction of an important historical work. Alpha Editions uses the
best technology to reproduce historical work in the same manner it was first
published to preserve its original nature. Any marks or number seen are left
intentionally to preserve its true form.

Contents

VOL III.

CHAPTER I.

AFTER THE SERMON.

As the sermon drew to a close, and the mist of his emotion began to disperse, individual faces of his audience again dawned out on the preacher's ken. Mr. Drew's head was down. As I have always said, certain things he had been taught in his youth, and had practised in his manhood, certain mean ways counted honest enough in the trade, had become to him, regarded from the ideal point of the divine in merchandize—such a merchandize, namely, as the share the son of man might have taken in buying and selling, had his reputed father been a shop-keeper instead of a carpenter—absolutely hateful, and the memory of them intolerable. Nor did it relieve him much to remind himself of the fact, that he knew not to the full the nature of the advantages he took, for he knew that he had known them such as shrunk from the light, not coming thereto to be made manifest. He was now doing his best to banish them from his business, and yet they were a painful presence to his spirit—so grievous to be borne, that the prospect held out by the preacher of an absolute and final deliverance from them by the indwelling presence of the God of all living men and true merchants, was a blessedness unspeakable. Small was the suspicion in the Abbey Church of Olaston that morning, that the well-known successful man of business was weeping. Who could once have imagined another reason for the laying of that round, good-humoured, contented face down on the book-board, than pure drowsiness from lack of work-day interest! Yet there was a human soul crying out after its birthright. Oh, to be clean as a mountain-river! clean as the air above the clouds, or on the middle seas! as the throbbing aether that fills the gulf betwixt star and star!—nay, as the thought of the Son of Man himself, who, to make all things new and clean, stood up against the old battery of sin-sprung suffering, withstanding and enduring and stilling the recoil of the awful force wherewith his Father had launched the worlds, and given birth to human souls with wills that might become free as his own!

While Wingfold had been speaking in general terms, with the race in his mind's, and the congregation in his body's eye, he had yet thought more of one soul, with its one crime and its intolerable burden, than all the rest: Leopold was ever present to him, and while he strove to avoid absorption in a personal interest however justifiable, it was of necessity that the thought of the most burdened sinner he knew should colour the whole of his utterance. At times indeed he felt as if he were speaking to him immediately—and to him only; at others, although then he saw her no more than him, that he was comforting the sister individually, in holding out to her brother the mighty hope of a restored purity. And when once more his mind could receive the messages brought home by his eyes, he saw upon Helen's face the red sunset of a rapt listening. True it was already fading away, but the eyes had wept, the glow yet hung about cheek and forehead, and the firm mouth had forgotten itself into a tremulous form, which the stillness of absorption had there for the moment fixed.

But even already, although he could not yet read it upon her countenance, a snake had begun to lift its head from the chaotic swamp which runs a creek at least into every soul, the rudimentary desolation, a remnant of the time when the world was without form and void. And the snake said: "Why, then, did he not speak like that to my Leopold? Why did he not comfort him with such a good hope, well-becoming a priest of the gentle Jesus? Or, if he fancied he must speak of confession, why did he not speak of it in plain honest terms, instead of suggesting the idea of it so that the poor boy imagined it came from his own spirit, and must therefore be obeyed as the will of God?"

So said the snake, and by the time Helen had walked home with her aunt, the glow had sunk from her soul, and a gray wintry mist had settled down upon her spirit. And she said to herself that if this last hope in George should fail her, she would not allow the matter to trouble her any farther; she was a free woman, and as Leopold had chosen other counsellors, had thus declared her unworthy of confidence, and, after all that she had suffered and done for love of him, had turned away from her, she would put money in her purse, set out for France or Italy, and leave him to the fate, whatever it might be, which his new advisers and his own obstinacy might bring upon him. Was the innocent bound to share the shame of the guilty? Had she not done enough? Would even her father require more of her than she had already done and endured?

When, therefore, she went into Leopold's room, and his eyes sought her from the couch, she took no notice that he had got up and dressed while she was at church; and he knew that a cloud had come between them, and that after all she had borne and done for him, he and his sister were now farther apart, for the time at least, than when oceans lay betwixt their birth and their meeting; and he found himself looking back with vague longing even to the terrible old house of Glaston, and the sharing of their agony therein. His eyes followed her as she walked across to the dressing-room, and the tears rose and filled them, but he said nothing. And the sister who, all the time of the sermon, had been filled with wave upon wave of wishing—that Poldie could hear this, could hear that, could have such a thought to comfort him, such a lovely word to drive the horror from his soul, now cast on him a chilly glance, and said never a word of the things to which she had listened with such heavings of the spirit-ocean; for she felt, with an instinct more righteous than her will, that they would but strengthen him in his determination to do whatever the teacher of them might approve. As she repassed him to go to the drawing-room, she did indeed say a word of kindness; but it was in a forced tone, and was only about his dinner! His eyes over-flowed, but he shut his lips so tight that his mouth grew grim with determination, and no more tears came.

To the friend who joined her at the church-door, and, in George Bascombe's absence, walked with them along Pine Street, Mrs. Ramshorn remarked that the curate was certainly a most dangerous man—particularly for young people to hear—he so confounded all the landmarks of right and wrong, representing the honest man as no better than the thief, and the murderer as no worse than anybody else—teaching people in fact that the best thing they could do was to commit some terrible crime, in order thereby to attain to a better innocence than without it could ever be theirs. How far she mistook, or how far she knew or suspected that she spoke falsely, I will not pretend to know. But although she spoke as she did, there was something, either in the curate or in the sermon, that had quieted her a little, and she was less contemptuous in her condemnation of him than usual.

Happily both for himself and others, the curate was not one of those who cripple the truth and blind their own souls by

> some craven scruple
> Of thinking too precisely on the event—
> A thought which, quartered, hath but one part wisdom,
> And ever three parts coward;

and hence, in proportion as he roused the honest, he gave occasion to the dishonest to cavil and condemn. Imagine St. Paul having a prevision of how he would be misunderstood, AND HEEDING IT!—what would then have become of all those his most magnificent outbursts? And would any amount of apostolic carefulness have protected him? I suspect it would only have given rise to more vulgar misunderstandings and misrepresentations still. To explain to him who loves not, is but to give him the more plentiful material for misinterpretation. Let a man have truth in the inward parts, and out of the abundance of his heart let his mouth speak. If then he should have ground to fear honest misunderstanding, let him preach again to enforce the truth for which he is jealous, and if it should seem to any that the two utterances need reconciling, let those who would have them consistent reconcile them for themselves.

The reason of George Bascombe's absence from church that morning was, that, after an early breakfast, he had mounted Helen's mare, and set out to call on Mr. Hooker before he should have gone to church. Helen expected him back to dinner, and was anxiously looking for him. So also was Leopold, but the hopes of the two were different.

At length the mare's hoofs echoed through all Sunday Glaston, and presently George rode up. The groom took his horse in the street, and he came into the drawing-room. Helen hastened to meet him.

"Well, George?" she said, anxiously.

"Oh, it's all right!—will be at least, I am sure. I will tell you all about it in the garden after dinner.—Aunt has the good sense never to interrupt us there," he added. "I'll just run and show myself to Leopold: he must not suspect that I am of your party and playing him false. Not that it is false, you know! for two negatives make a positive, and to fool a mad-man is to give him fair play."

The words jarred sorely on Helen's ear.

Bascombe hurried to Leopold, and informed him that he had seen Mr. Hooker, and that all was arranged for taking him over to his place on Tuesday morning, if by that time he should be able for the journey.

"Why not to-morrow?" said Leopold. "I am quite able."

"Oh! I told him you were not very strong. And he wanted a run after the hounds to-morrow. So we judged it better put off till Tuesday."

Leopold gave a sigh, and said no more.

CHAPTER II.

BASCOMBE AND THE MAGISTRATE.

After dinner, the cousins went to the summer-house, and there George gave Helen his report, revealing his plan and hope for Leopold.

"Such fancies must be humoured, you know, Helen. There is nothing to be gained by opposing them," he said.

Helen looked at him with keen eyes, and he returned the gaze. The confidence betwixt them was not perfect: each was doubtful as to the thought of the other, and neither asked what it was.

"A fine old cock is Mr. Hooker!" said Greorge; "a jolly, good-natured, brick-faced squire; a tory of course, and a sound church-man; as simple as a baby, and took everything I told him without a hint of doubt or objection;—just the sort of man I expected to find him! When I mentioned my name, &c., he found he had known my father, and that gave me a good start. Then I lauded his avenue, and apologized for troubling him so early and on Sunday too, but said it was a pure work of mercy in which I begged his assistance—as a magistrate, I added, lest he should fancy I had come after a subscription. It was a very delicate case, I said, in which were concerned the children of a man of whom he had, I believed, at one time known something—General Lingard. 'To be sure!' he cried; 'knew him very well; a fine fellow—but hasty, sir—hasty in his temper!' I said I had never known him myself, but one of his children was my cousin; the other was the child of his second wife, a Hindoo lady unfortunately, and it was about him I presumed to trouble him. Then I plunged into the matter at once, telling him that Leopold had had violent brain-fever, brought on by a horrible drug, the use of which, if use I dare call it, he had learnt in India; and that, although he had recovered from the fever, it was very doubtful if ever he would recover from the consequences of it, for that he had become the prey of a fixed idea, the hard deposit from a heated imagination. 'And pray what is the idea?' he asked. 'Neither more nor less,' I answered, 'than that he is a murderer!'—'God bless me!' he cried, somewhat to my alarm, for I had been making all this preamble to prejudice the old gentleman in the right direction, lest afterwards Leopold's plausibility might be too much for him. So I echoed the spirit of his exclamation, declaring it was one of the saddest things I had ever known, that a fellow of such sweet and gentle nature, one utterly incapable of unkindness, not to say violence, should be so possessed by misery and remorse for a phantom-deed, no more his than if he had dreamed it, a thing he not only did not do, but never could have done. I had not yet however told him, I said, what was perhaps the saddest point in the whole sad story— namely, that the attack had been brought on by the news of the actual murder of a lady to whom he had been passionately attached; the horror of it had unhinged his reason, then turned and fastened upon his imagination; so that he was now convinced beyond the reach of argument or even the clearest proof, that it was his own hand that drove the knife to her heart. Then I recalled to his memory the case as reported, adding that the fact of the murderer's prolonged evasion of justice, appeared, by some curious legerdemain of his excited fancy, if not to have suggested— of that I was doubtful—yet to have ripened his conviction of guilt. Now nothing would serve him but he must give himself up, confess—no, that was not a true word in his case!—accuse himself of the crime, and meet his fate on the gallows,— 'in the hope, observe, my dear sir,' I said, 'of finding her in the other world, and there making it up with her!'—'God bless me!' he cried again, in a tone of absolute horror. And every now and then, while I spoke, he would ejaculate something; and still as he listened his eyes grew more and more bloodshot with interest and compassion. 'Ah, I see!' he said then; 'you want to send him to a madhouse?—Don't do it,' he continued, in a tone of expostulation, almost entreaty. 'Poor boy! He may get over it. Let his friends look to him. He has a sister, you say?' I quickly reassured him, telling him such was no one's desire, and saying I would come to the point in a moment, only there was one thing more which had interested me greatly, as revealing how a brain in such a condition will befool itself, all but generating two individualities.—There I am afraid I put my foot in it, but he was far too simple to see it was cloven—ha! ha! and I hastened to remark that, as a magistrate, he must have numberless opportunities of noting similar phenomena. He waved his hand in deprecation, and I hastened to remark that, up to a certain point, whatever hint the newspapers had given, Leopold had expanded and connected with every other, but that at one part of the story I had found him entirely at fault: he could not tell what he did, where he went, or how he had felt, first after the deed was done. He confessed all after that was a blank until he found himself in bed. But when I told him something he had not seen—which his worship might remember—the testimony namely of the coast-guardsmen—about the fishing-boat with the two men in it—I had here to refresh his memory as to the whole of that circumstance—and did so by handing him the newspaper containing it—that was what I made you give me the paper for—I have lost the thread of my sentence, but never mind. I told him then something I have not told you yet, Helen, namely, that when I happened to allude to that portion of the story, Leopold started up with flashing eyes, and exclaimed, 'Now I remember! It all comes back to me as clear as day. I remember running down the hill, and jumping into the boat just as they shoved off. I was exhausted, and fell down in the stern. When I came to myself, the two men were forward: I saw their legs beneath the sails. I thought they would be sure to give me up, and at once I slipped overboard. The water revived me, but when I reached the shore, I fell down again, and lay there I don't know how long. Indeed I don't remember anything more except very confusedly.' That is what Leopold said, and what I now told Mr. Hooker. Then at last I opened my mind to him as to wherein I ventured to ask his assistance; and my petition was, that he would allow me to bring Leopold, and would let him go through the form of giving himself up to justice. Especially I begged that he would listen to all he had to say, and give no sign that he doubted his story. 'And then, sir,' I concluded, 'I would leave it to you to do what we cannot—reconcile him to going home instead of to prison.'

"He sat with his head on his hand for a while, as if pondering some weighty question of law. Then he said suddenly: 'It is now almost church-time. I will think the matter over. You may rely upon me. Will you take a seat in my pew and dine with us after?' I excused myself on the ground that I must return at once to poor Leopold, who was anxiously looking for me. And you must forgive me, Helen, and not fancy me misusing Fanny, if I did yield to the temptation of a little longer ride. I have scarcely more than walked her, with a canter now and then when we had the chance of a bit of turf."

Helen assured him with grateful eyes that she knew Fanny was as safe with him as with herself; and she felt such a gush of gratitude follow the revival of hope, that she was nearer being in love with her cousin to ever before. Her gratitude inwardly delighted George, and he thought the light in her blue eyes lovelier than ever; but although strougly tempted, he judged it better to delay a formal confession until circumstances should be more comfortable.

CHAPTER III.

THE CONFESSION.

All that and the following day Leopold was in spirits for him wonderful. On Monday night there came a considerable reaction; he was dejected, worn, and weary. Twelve o'clock the next day was the hour appointed for their visit to Mr. Hooker, and at eleven he was dressed and ready—restless, agitated, and very pale, but not a whit less determined than at first. A drive was the pretext for borrowing Mrs. Ramshorn's carriage.

"Why is Mr. Wingfold not coming?" asked Lingard, anxiously, when it began to move.

"I fancy we shall be quite as comfortable without him, Poldie," said Helen. "Did you expect him?"

"He promised to go with me. But he hasn't called since the time was fixed."—Here Helen looked out of the window.—"I can't think why it is. I can do my duty without him though," continued Leopold, "and perhaps it is just as well.—Do you know, George, since I made up my mind, I have seen her but once, and that was last night, and only in a dream."

"A state of irresolution is one peculiarly open to unhealthy impressions," said George, good-naturedly disposing of his long legs so that they should be out of the way.

Leopold turned from him to his sister.

"The strange thing, Helen," he said, "was that I did not feel the least afraid of her, or even abashed before her. 'I see you,' I said. 'Be at peace. I am coming; and you shall do to me what you will.' And then—what do you think?—O my God! she smiled one of her own old smiles, only sad too, very sad, and vanished. I woke, and she seemed only to have just left the room, for there was a stir in the darkness.—Do you believe in ghosts, George?"

Leopold was not one of George's initiated, I need hardly say.

"No," answered Bascombe.

"I don't wonder. I can't blame you, for neither did I once. But just wait till you have made one, George!"

"God forbid!" exclaimed Bascombe, a second time forgetting himself.

"Amen!" said Leopold: "for after that there's no help but be one yourself, you know."

"If he would only talk like that to old Hooker!" thought George. "It would go a long way to forestall any possible misconception of the case."

"I can't think why Mr. Wingfold did not come yesterday," resumed Leopold. "I made sure he would."

"Now, Poldie, you mustn't talk," said Helen, "or you'll be exhausted before we get to Mr. Hooker's."

"She did not wish the non-appearance of the curate on Monday to be closely inquired into. His company at the magistrate's was by all possible means to be avoided. George had easily persuaded Helen, more easily than he expected, to wait their return in the carriage, and the two men were shown into the library, where the magistrate presently joined them. He would have shaken hands with Leopold as well as George, but the conscious felon drew back.

"No, sir; excuse me," he said. "Hear what I have to tell you first; and if after that you will shake hands with me, it will be a kindness indeed. But you will not! you will not!"

Worthy Mr. Hooker was overwhelmed with pity at sight of the worn sallow face with the great eyes, in which he found every appearance confirmatory of the tale wherewith Bascombe had filled and prejudiced every fibre of his judgment. He listened in the kindest way while the poor boy forced the words of his confession from his throat. But Leopold never dreamed of attributing his emotion to any other cause than compassion for one who had been betrayed into such a crime. It was against his will, for he seemed now bent, even to unreason, on fighting every weakness, that he was prevailed upon to take a little wine. Having ended, he sat silent, in the posture of one whose wrists are already clasped by the double bracelet of steel.

Now Mr. Hooker had thought the thing out in church on the Sunday; and after a hard run at the tail of a strong fox over a rough country on the Monday, and a good sleep well into the morning of the Tuesday, could see no better way. His device was simple enough.

"My dear young gentleman," he said, "I am very sorry for you, but I must do my duty."

"That, sir, is what I came to you for," answered Leopold, humbly.

"Then you must consider yourself my prisoner. The moment you, are gone, I shall make notes of your deposition, and proceed to arrange for the necessary formalities. As a mere matter of form, I shall take your own bail in a thousand pounds to surrender when called upon."

"But I am not of age, and haven't got a thousand pounds," said Leopold.

"Perhaps Mr. Hooker will accept my recognizance in the amount?" said Bascombe.

"Certainly," answered Mr. Hooker, and wrote something, which Bascombe signed.

"You are very good, George," said Leopold. "But you know I can't run away if I would," he added with a pitiful attempt at a smile.

"I hope you will soon be better," said the magistrate kindly.

"Why such a wish, sir?" returned Leopold, almost reproachfully, and the good man stood abashed before him.

He thought of it afterwards, and was puzzled to know how it was.

"You must hold yourself in readiness," he said, recovering himself with an effort, "to give yourself up at any moment. And, rememher, I shall call upon you when I please, every week, perhaps, or oftener, to see that you are safe. Your aunt is an old friend of mine, and there will be no need of explanations. This turns out to be no common case, and after hearing the whole, I do not hesitate to offer you my hand."

Leopold was overcome by his kindness, and withdrew speechless, but greatly relieved.

Several times during the course of his narrative, its apparent truthfulness and its circumstantiality went nigh to stagger Mr. Hooker; but a glance at Bascombe's face, with its half-amused smile, instantly set him right again, and he thought with dismay how near he had been to letting himself be fooled by a madman.

Again in the carriage, Leopold laid his head on Helen's shoulder, and looked up in her face with such a smile as she had never seen on his before. Certainly there was something in confession—if only enthusiasts like Mr. Wingfold would not spoil all by pushing things to extremes and turning good into bad!

Leopold was yet such a child, had so little occupied himself with things about him, and had been so entirely taken up with his passion, and the poetry of existence unlawfully forced, that if his knowledge of the circumstances of Emmeline's murder had depended on the newspapers, he would have remained in utter ignorance concerning them. From the same causes he was so entirely unacquainted with the modes of criminal procedure, that the conduct of the magistrate never struck him as strange, not to say illegal. And so strongly did he feel the good man's kindness and sympathy, that his comfort from making a clean breast of it was even greater than he expected. Before they reached home he was fast asleep. When laid on his couch, he almost fell asleep again, and Helen saw him smile as he slept.

CHAPTER IV.

THE MASK.

But although such was George Bascombe's judgment of Leopold, and such his conduct of his affair, he could not prevent the recurrent intrusion of the flickering doubt which had showed itself when first he listened to the story. Amid all the wildness of the tale there was yet a certain air, not merely of truthfulness in the narrator—that was not to be questioned—but of verisimilitude in the narration, which had its effect, although it gave rise to no conscious exercise of discriminating or ponderating faculty. Leopold's air of conviction also, although of course that might well accompany the merest invention rooted in madness, yet had its force, persistently as George poohpoohed it—which he did the more strenuously from the intense, even morbid abhorrence of his nature to being taken in, and having to confess himself of unstable intellectual equilibrium. Possibly this was not the only kind of thing in which the sensitiveness of a vanity he would himself have disowned, had rendered him unfit for perceiving the truth. Nor do I know how much there may be to choose between the two shames—that of accepting what is untrue, and that of refusing what is true.

The second time he listened to Leopold's continuous narrative, the doubt returned with more clearness and less flicker: there was such a thing as being over-wise: might he not be taking himself in with his own incredulity? Ought he not to apply some test? And did Leopold's story offer any means of doing so?—One thing, he then found, had been dimly haunting his thoughts ever since he heard it: Leopold affirmed that he had thrown his cloak and mask down an old pit-shaft, close by the place of murder: if there was such a shaft, could it be searched?—Recurring doubt at length so wrought upon his mind, that he resolved to make his holiday excursion to that neighbourhood, and there endeavour to gain what assurance of any sort might be to be had. What end beyond his own possible satisfaction the inquiry was to answer he did not ask himself. The restless spirit of the detective, so often conjoined with indifference to what is in its own nature true, was at work in him—but that was not all: he must know the very facts, if possible, of whatever concerned Helen. I shall not follow his proceedings closely: it is with their reaction upon Leopold that I have to do.

The house where the terrible thing took place was not far from a little moorland village. There Bascombe found a small inn, where he took up his quarters, pretending to be a geologist out for a holiday. He soon came upon the disused shaft.

The inn was a good deal frequented in the evenings by the colliers of the district—a rough race, but not beyond the influences of such an address, mingled of self-assertion and good fellowship, as Bascombe brought to bear upon them, for he had soon perceived that amongst them he might find the assistance he wanted. In the course of conversation, therefore, he mentioned the shaft, on which he pretended to have come in his rambles. Remarking on the danger of such places, he learned that this one served for ventilation, and was still accessible below from other workings. Thereafter he begged permission to go down one of the pits, on pretext of examining the coal-strata, and having secured for his guide one of the most intelligent of those whose acquaintance he had made at the inn, persuaded him, partly by expressions of incredulity because of the distance between, to guide him to the bottom of the shaft whose accessibility he maintained. That they were going in the right direction, he had the testimony of the little compass he carried at his watch-chain, and at length he saw a faint gleam before him. When at last he raised his head, wearily bent beneath the low roofs of the passages, and looked upwards, there was a star looking down at him out of the sky of day! But George never wasted time in staring at what was above his head, and so began instantly to search about as if examining the indications of the strata. Was it possible? Could it be? There was a piece of black something that was not coal, and seemed textile! It was a half-mask, for there were the eye-holes in it! He caught it up and hurried it into his bag—not so quickly but that the haste set his guide speculating. And Bascombe saw that the action was noted. The man afterwards offered to carry his bag, but he would not allow him.

The next morning he left the place and returned to London, taking Glaston, by a detour, on his way. A few questions to Leopold drew from him a description of the mask he had worn, entirely corresponding with the one George had found; and at length he was satisfied that there was truth more than a little in Leopold's confession. It was not his business, however, he now said to himself, to set magistrates right. True, he had set Mr. Hooker wrong in the first place, but he had done it in good faith, and how could he turn traitor to Helen and her brother? Besides, he was sure the magistrate himself would be anything but obliged to him for opening his eyes! At the same time Leopold's fanatic eagerness after confession might drive the matter further, and if so, it might become awkward for him. He might be looked to for the defence, and were he not certain that his guide had marked his concealment of what he had picked up, he might have ventured to undertake it, for certainly it would have been a rare chance for a display of the forensic talent he believed himself to possess; but as it was, the moment he was called to the bar—which would be within a fortnight—he would go abroad, say to Paris, and there, for twelve months or so, await events.

When he disclosed to Helen his evil success in the coalpit, it was but the merest film of a hope it destroyed, for she KNEW that her brother was guilty.

George and she now felt that they were linked by the possession of a common, secret.

But the cloak had been found a short time before, and was in the possession of Emmeline's mother. That mother was a woman of strong passions and determined character. The first shock of the catastrophe over, her grief was almost supplanted by a rage for vengeance, in the compassing of which no doubt she vaguely imagined she would be doing something to right her daughter. Hence the protracted concealment of the murderer was bitterness to her soul, and she vowed herself to discovery and revenge as the one business of her life. In this her husband, a good deal broken by the fearful event, but still more by misfortunes of another kind which had begun to threaten him, offered her no assistance, and indeed felt neither her passion urge him, nor her perseverance hold him to the pursuit.

In the neighbourhood her mind was well known, and not a few found their advantage in supplying her passion with the fuel of hope. Any hint of evidence, however small, the remotest suggestion even towards discovery, they would carry at once to her, for she was an open-handed woman, and in such case would give with a profusion that, but for the feeling concerned, would have been absurd, and did expose her to the greed of every lying mendicant within reach of her. Not unnaturally, therefore, it had occurred to a certain collier to make his way to the bottom of the shaft, on the chance— hardly of finding, but of being enabled to invent something worth reporting; and there, to the very fooling of his barren expectation, he had found the cloak.

The mother had been over to Holland, where she had instituted unavailing inquiries in the villages along the coast and among the islands, and had been home but a few days when the cloak was carried to her. In her mind it immediately associated itself with the costumes of the horrible ball, and at once she sought the list of her guests thereat. It was before her at the very moment when the man, who had been Bascombe's guide, sent in to request an interview, the result of which was to turn her attention for the time in another direction.—Who might the visitor to the mine have been?

Little was to be gathered in the neighbourhood beyond the facts that the letters G. B. were on his carpet-bag, and that a scrap of torn envelope bore what seemed the letters mple. She despatched the poor indications to an inquiry-office in London.

CHAPTER V.

FURTHER DECISION.

The day after his confession to Mr. Hooker, a considerable re-action took place in Lingard. He did not propose to leave his bed, and lay exhausted. He said he had caught cold. He coughed a little; wondered why Mr. Wingfold did not come to see him, dozed a good deal, and often woke with a start. Mrs. Ramshorn thought Helen ought to make him get up: nothing, she said, could be worse for him than lying in bed; but Helen thought, even if her aunt were right, he must be humoured. The following day Mr. Hooker called, inquired after him, and went up to his room to see him. There he said all he could think of to make him comfortable; repeated that certain preliminaries had to be gone through before the commencement of the prosecution; said that while these went on, it was better he should be in his sister's care than in prison, where, if he went at once, he most probably would die before the trial came on; that in the meantime he was responsible for him; that, although he had done quite right in giving himself up, he must not let what was done and could no more be helped, prey too much upon his mind, lest it should render him unable to give his evidence with proper clearness, and he should be judged insane and sent to Broadmoor, which would be frightful. He ended by saying that he had had great provocation, and that he was certain the judge would consider it in passing sentence, only he must satisfy the jury there had been no premeditation.

"I will not utter a word to excuse myself, Mr. Hooker," replied Leopold.

The worthy magistrate smiled sadly, and went away, if possible, more convinced of the poor lad's insanity.

The visit helped Leopold over that day, but when the next also passed, and neither did Wingfold appear, nor any explanation of his absence reach him, he made up his mind to act again for himself.

The cause of the curate's apparent neglect, though ill to find, was not far to seek.

On the Monday, he had, upon some pretext or other, been turned away; on the Tuesday, he had been told that Mr. Lingard had gone for a drive; on the Wednesday, that he was much too tired to be seen; and thereupon had at length judged it better to leave things to right themselves. If Leopold did not want to see him, it would be of no use by persistence to force his way to him; while on the other hand, if he did want to see him, he felt convinced the poor fellow would manage to have his own way somehow.

The next morning after he had thus resolved, Leopold declared himself better, and got up and dressed. He then lay on the sofa and waited as quietly as he could until Helen went out—Mr, Faber insisting she should do so every day. It was no madness, but a burning desire for life, coupled with an utter carelessness of that which is commonly called life, that now ruled his behaviour. He tied his slippers on his feet, put on his smoking-cap, crept unseen from the house, and took the direction, of the Abbey. The influence of the air—by his weakness rendered intoxicating, the strange look of everything around him, the nervous excitement of every human approach, kept him up until he reached the churchyard, across which he was crawling, to find the curate's lodging, when suddenly his brain seemed to go swimming away into regions beyond the senses. He attempted to seat himself on a grave-stone, but lost consciousness, and fell at full length between that and the next one.

When Helen returned, she was horrified to find that he had gone—when, or whither nobody knew: no one had missed him. Her first fear was the river, but her conscience enlightened her, and her shame could not prevent her from seeking him at the curate's. In her haste she passed him where he lay.

Shown into the curate's study, she gave a hurried glance around, and her anxiety became terror again.

"Oh! Mr. Wingfold," she cried, "where is Leopold?"

"I have not seen him," replied the curate, turning pale.

"Then he has thrown himself in the river!" cried Helen, and sank on a chair.

The curate caught up his hat.

"You wait here," he said. "I will go and look for him."

But Helen rose, and, without another word, they set off together, and again entered the churchyard. As they hurried across it, the curate caught sight of something on the ground, and, springing forward, found Leopold.

"He is dead!" cried Helen, in an agony, when she saw him stop and stoop.

He looked dead indeed; but what appalled her the most reassured Wingfold a little: blood had flowed freely from a cut on his eyebrow.

The curate lifted him, no hard task, out of the damp shadow, and laid him on the stone, which was warm in the sun, with his head on Helen's lap, then ran to order the carriage, and hastened back with brandy. They got a little into his mouth, but he could not swallow it. Still it seemed to do him good, for presently he gave a deep sigh; and just then they heard the carriage stop at the gate. Wingfold took him up, carried him to it, got in with him in his arms, and held him on his knees until he reached the manor house, when he carried him upstairs and laid him on the sofa. When they had brought him round a little, he undressed him and put him to bed.

"Do not leave me," murmured Leopold, just as Helen entered the room, and she heard it.

Wingfold looked to her for the answer he was to make. Her bearing was much altered: she was both ashamed and humbled.

"Yes, Leopold," she said, "Mr. Wingfold will, I am sure, stay with you as long as he can."

"Indeed I will," assented the curate. "But I must run for Mr. Faber first."

"How did I come here?" asked Leopold, opening his eyes large upon Helen after swallowing a spoonful of the broth she held to his lips.

But, before she could answer him, he turned sick, and by the time the doctor came was very feverish. Faber gave the necessary directions, and Wingfold walked back with him to get his prescription made up.

CHAPTER VI.

THE CURATE AND THE DOCTOR.

"There is something strange about that young man's illness," said Faber, as soon as they had left the house. "I fancy you know more than you can tell, and if so, then I have committed no indiscretion in saying as much."

"Perhaps it might be an indiscretion to acknowledge as much however," said the curate with a smile.

"You are right. I have not been long in the place," returned Faber, "and you had no opportunity of testing me. But I am indifferent honest as well as you, though I don't go you in everything."

"People would have me believe you don't go with me in anything."

"They say as much—do they?" returned Faber with some annoyance. "I thought I had been careful not to trespass on your preserves."

"As for preserves, I don't know of any," answered the curate. "There is no true bird in the grounds that won't manage somehow to escape the snare of the fowler."

"Well," said the doctor, "I know nothing about God and all that kind of thing, but, though I don't think I'm a coward exactly either, I know I should like to have your pluck."

"I haven't got any pluck," said the curate.

"Tell that to the marines," said Faber. "I daren't go and say what I think or don't think, even in the bedroom of my least orthodox patient—at least, if I do, I instantly repent it—while you go on saying what you really believe Sunday after Sunday!—How you can believe it, I don't know, and it's no business of mine."

"Oh yes, it is!" returned Wingfold. "But as to the pluck, it may be a man's duty to say in the pulpit what he would be just as wrong to say by a sick-bed."

"That has nothing to do with the pluck! That's all I care about."

"It has everything to do with what you take for pluck. My pluck is only Don Worm."

"I don't know what you mean by that."

"It's Benedick's name, in Much Ado about Nothing, for the conscience. MY pluck is nothing but my conscience."

"It's a damned fine thing to have anyhow, whatever name you put upon it!" said Faber.

"Excuse me if I find your epithet more amusing than apt," said Wingfold, laughing.

"You are quite right," said Faber. "I apologize."

"As to the pluck again," Wingfold resumed, "—if you think of this one fact—that my whole desire is to believe in God, and that the only thing I can be sure of sometimes is that, if there be a God, none but an honest man will ever find him, you will not then say there is much pluck in my speaking the truth?"

"I don't see that that makes it a hair easier, in the face of such a set of gaping noodles as—"

"I beg your pardon:—there is more lack of conscience than of brains in the Abbey of a Sunday, I fear."

"Well, all I have to say is, I can't for the life of me see what you want to believe in a God for! It seems to me the world would go rather better without any such fancy. Look here now: there is young Spenser—out there at Harwood—a patient of mine. His wife died yesterday—one of the loveliest young creatures you ever saw. The poor fellow is as bad about it as fellow can be. Well, he's one of your sort, and said to me the other day, just as you would have him, 'It's the will of God,' he said, 'and we must hold our peace.'—'Don't talk to me about God,' I said, for I couldn't stand it. 'Do you mean to tell me that, if there was a God, he would have taken such a lovely creature as that away from her husband and her helpless infant, at the age of two and twenty? I scorn to believe it.'"

"What did he say to that?"

"He turned as white as death, and said never a word."

"Ah, you forgot that you were taking from him his only hope of seeing her again!"

"I certainly did not think of that," said Faber.

"Even then," resumed Wingfold, "I should not say you were wrong, if you were prepared to add that you had searched every possible region of existence, and had found no God; or that you had tried every theory man had invented, or even that you were able to invent yourself, and had found none of them consistent with the being of a God. I do not say that then you would be right in your judgment, for another man, of equal weight, might have had a different experience. I only say, I would not then blame you. But you must allow it a very serious thing to assert as a conviction, without such grounds as the assertor has pretty fully satisfied himself concerning, what COULD only drive the sting of death ten times deeper."

The doctor was silent.

"I doubt not you spoke in a burst of indignation; but it seems to me the indignation of a man unaccustomed to ponder the things concerning which he expresses such a positive conviction."

"You are wrong there," returned Faber; "for I was brought up in the straitest sect of the Pharisees, and know what I am saying."

"The straitest sect of the Pharisees can hardly be the school in which to gather any such idea of a God as one could wish to be a reality."

"They profess to know."

"Is that any argument of weight, they and their opinions being what they are?—If there be a God, do you imagine he would choose any strait sect under the sun to be his interpreters?"

"But the question is not of the idea of a God, but of the existence of any, seeing, if he exists, he must be such as the human heart could never accept as God, inasmuch as he at least permits, if not himself enacts cruelty. My argument to poor Spenser remains—however unwise or indeed cruel it may have been."

"I grant it a certain amount of force—as much exactly as had gone to satisfy the children whom I heard the other day agreeing that Dr. Faber was a very cruel man, for he pulled out nurse's tooth, and gave poor little baby such a nasty, nasty powder!"

"Is that a fair parallel? I must look at it."

"I think it is. What you do is often unpleasant, sometimes most painful, but it does not follow that you are a cruel man, and a hurter instead of a healer of men."

"I think there is a fault in the analogy," said Faber. "For here am I nothing but a slave to laws already existing, and compelled to work according to them. It is not my fault therefore that the remedies I have to use are unpleasant. But if there be a God, he has the matter in his own hands."

"There is weight and justice in your argument, which may well make the analogy appear at first sight false. But is there no theory possible that should make it perfect?"

"I do not see how there should be any. For, if you say God is under any such compulsion as I am under, then surely the house is divided against itself, and God is not God any more."

"For my part," said the curate, "I think I COULD believe in a God who did but his imperfect best: in one all power, and not all goodness, I could not believe. But suppose that the design of God involved the perfecting of men as the CHILDREN OF GOD—'I said ye are gods,'—that he would have them partakers of his own blessedness in kind—be as himself;—suppose his grand idea could not be contented with creatures perfect ONLY by his gift, so far as that should reach, and having no willing causal share in the perfection, that is, partaking not at all of God's individuality and free-will and choice of good; then suppose that suffering were the only way through which the individual could be set, in separate and self-individuality, so far apart from God, that it might WILL, and so become a partaker of his singleness and freedom;—and suppose that this suffering must be and had been initiated by God's taking his share, and that the infinitely greater share;—suppose next, that God saw the germ of a pure affection, say in your friend and his wife, but saw also that it was a germ so imperfect and weak that it could not encounter the coming frosts and winds of the world without loss and decay, while, if they were parted now for a few years, it would grow and strengthen and expand, to the certainty of an infinitely higher and deeper and keener love through the endless ages to follow—so that by suffering should come, in place of contented decline, abortion, and death, a troubled birth of joyous result in health and immortality;—suppose all this, and what then?"

Faber was silent a moment, then answered,

"Your theory has but one fault: it is too good to be true."

"My theory leaves plenty of difficulty, but has no such fault as that. Why, what sort of a God would content you, Mr. Faber? The one idea is too bad, the other too good to be true. Must you expand and pare until you get one exactly to the measure of yourself ere you can accept it as thinkable or possible? Why, a less God than that would not rest your soul a week. The only possibility of believing in a God seems to me to lie in finding an idea of a God large enough, grand enough, pure enough, lovely enough to be fit to believe in."

"And have you found such—may I ask?"

"I think I am finding such."

"Where?"

"In the man of the New Testament. I have thought a little more about these things, I fancy, than you have, Mr. Faber. I may come to be sure of something; I don't see how a man can ever be sure of NOTHING."

"Don't suppose me quite dumbfoundered, though I can't answer you off hand," said Mr. Faber, as they reached his door.—"Come in with me, and I will make up the medicine myself; it will save time. There are a thousand difficulties," he resumed in the surgery, "some of them springing from peculiar points that come before one of my profession, which I doubt if you would be able to meet so readily. But about this poor fellow, Lingard. You know Glaston gossip says he is out of his mind."

"If I were you, Mr. Faber, I would not take pains to contradict it. He is not out of his mind, but has such trouble in it as might well drive him out.— Don't you even hint at that, though."

"I understand," said Faber.

"If doctor and minister did understand each other and work together," said Wingfold, "I fancy a good deal more might be done."

"I don't doubt it.—What sort of fellow is that cousin of theirs—Bascombe is his name, I believe?"

"A man to suit you, I should think," said the curate; "a man with a most tremendous power of believing in nothing."

"Come, come!" returned the doctor, "you don't know half enough about me to tell what sort of man I should like or dislike."

"Well, all I will say more of Bascombe is, that if he were not conceited he would be honest; and if he were as honest as he believes himself, he would not be so ready to judge every one dishonest who does not agree with him."

"I hope we may have another talk soon," said the doctor, searching for a cork. "Some day I will tell you a few things that may stagger you."

"Likely enough: I am only learning to walk yet," said Wingfold. "But a man may stagger and not fall, and I am ready to hear anything you choose to tell me."

Faber handed him the bottle, and he took his leave.

CHAPTER VII.

HELEN AND THE CURATE.

Before the morning Leopold lay wound in the net of a low fever, almost as ill as ever, but with this difference, that his mind was far less troubled, and that even his most restless dreams no longer scared him awake to a still nearer assurance of misery. And yet, many a time, as she watched by his side, it was excruciatingly plain to Helen that the stuff of which his dreams were made was the last process to the final execution of the law. She thought she could follow it all in his movements and the expressions of his countenance. At a certain point, the cold dew always appeared on his forehead, after which invariably came a smile, and he would be quiet until near morning, when the same signs again appeared. Sometimes he would murmur prayers, and sometimes it seemed to Helen that he must fancy himself talking face to face with Jesus, for the look of blessed and trustful awe upon his countenance was amazing in its beauty.

For Helen herself, she was prey to a host of changeful emotions. At one time she accused herself bitterly of having been the cause of the return of his illness; the next a gush of gladness would swell her heart at the thought that now she had him at least safer for a while, and that he might die and so escape the whole crowd of horrible possibilities. For George's manipulation of the magistrate could but delay the disclosure of the truth; even should no discovery be made, Leopold must at length suspect a trick, and that would at once drive him to fresh action.

But amongst the rest, a feeling which had but lately begun to indicate its far-off presence now threatened to bring with it a deeper and more permanent sorrow: it became more and more plain to her that she had taken the evil part against the one she loved best in the world; that she had been as a Satan to him; had driven him back, stood almost bodily in the way to turn him from the path of peace. Whether the path he had sought to follow was the only one or not, it was the only one he knew; and that it was at least A true one, was proved by the fact that he had already found in it the beginnings of the peace he sought; while she, for the avoidance of shame and pity, for the sake of the family, as she had said to herself, had pursued a course which if successful, would at best have resulted in shutting him up, as in a madhouse, with his own inborn horrors, with vain remorse, and equally vain longing. Her conscience, now that her mind was quieter, from the greater distance to which the threatening peril had again withdrawn, had taken the opportunity of speaking louder. And she listened—but still with one question ever presented: Why might he not appropriate the consolations of the gospel without committing the suicide of surrender? She could not see that confession was the very door of refuge and safety, towards which he must press.

George's absence was now again a relief, and while she feared and shrank from the severity of Wingfold, she could not help a certain indiscribable sense of safety in his presence—at least so long as Leopold was too ill to talk.

For the curate, he became more and more interested in the woman who could love so strongly, and yet not entirely, who suffered and must still suffer so much, and who a faith even no greater than his own might render comparatively blessed. The desire to help her grew and grew in him, but he could see no way of reaching her. And then he began to discover one peculiar advantage belonging to the little open chamber of the pulpit—open not only or specially to heaven above, but to so many of the secret chambers of the souls of the congregation. For what a man dares not, could not if he dared, and dared not if he could, say to another, even at the time and in the place fittest of all, he can say thence, open-faced before the whole congregation; and the person in need thereof may hear it without umbrage, or the choking husk of individual application, irritating to the rejection of what truth may lie in it for him. Would that our pulpits were all in the power of such men as by suffering know the human, and by obedience the divine heart! Then would the office of instruction be no more mainly occupied by the press, but the faces of true men would everywhere be windows for the light of the Spirit to enter other men's souls, and the voice of their words would follow with the forms of what truth they saw, and the power of the Lord would speed from heart to heart. Then would men soon understand that not the form of even soundest words availeth anything, but a new creature.

When Wingfold was in the pulpit, then, he could speak as from the secret to the secret; but elsewhere he felt, in regard to Helen, like a transport-ship filled with troops, which must go sailing around the shores of an invaded ally, in frustrate search for a landing. Oh, to help that woman, that the light of life might go up in her heart, and her cheek bloom again with the rose of peace! But not a word could he speak in her presence, for he heard everything be would have said as he thought it would sound to her, and therefore he had no utterance. Is it an infirmity of certain kinds of men, or a wise provision for their protection, that the brightest forms the truth takes in their private cogitations seem to lose half their lustre and all their grace when uttered in the presence of an unreceptive nature, and they hear, as it were, their own voice reflected in a poor, dull, inharmonious echo, and are disgusted?

But, on the other hand, ever in the pauses of the rushing, ever in the watery gleams of life that broke through the clouds and drifts of the fever, Leopold sought his friend, and, finding him, shone into a brief radiance, or, missing him, gloomed back into the land of visions. The tenderness of the curate's service, the heart that showed itself in everything he did, even in the turn and expression of the ministering hand, was a kind of revelation to Helen. For while his intellect was hanging about the door, asking questions, and uneasily shifting hither and thither in its unloved perplexities, the spirit of the master had gone by it unseen, and entered into the chamber of his heart.

After preaching the sermon last recorded, there came a reaction of doubt and depression on the mind of the curate, greater than usual. Had he not gone farther than his right? Had he not implied more conviction than was his? Words could not go beyond his satisfaction with what he found in the gospel, or the hopes for the range of his conscious life springing therefrom; but was he not now making people suppose him more certain of the FACT of these things than he was? He was driven to console himself with the reflection that so long as he had had no such intention, even if he had been so carried away by the delight of his heart as to give such an impression, it mattered little: what was it to other people what he believed or how he believed? If he had not been untrue to himself, no harm would follow. Was a man never to talk from the highest in him to the forgetting of the lower? Was a man never to be carried beyond himself and the regions of his knowledge? If so, then farewell poetry and prophecy—yea, all grand discovery!—for things must be foreseen ere they can be realized—apprehended ere they be comprehended. This much he could say for himself, and no more, that he was ready to lay down his life for the mere CHANCE, if he might so use the word, of these things being true; nor did he argue any devotion in that, seeing life without them would be to him a waste of unreality. He could bear witness to no facts—but to the truth, to the loveliness and harmony and righteousness and safety that he saw in the idea of the Son of Man—as he read it in the story. He dared not say what, in a time of persecution, torture might work upon him, but he felt right hopeful that, even were he base enough to deny him, any cock might crow him back to repentance. At the same time he saw plain enough that even if he gave his body to be burned, it were no sufficing assurance of his Christianity: nothing could satisfy him of that less than the conscious presence of the perfect charity. Without that he was still outside the kingdom, wandering in a dream around its walls.

Difficulties went on presenting themselves; at times he would be overwhelmed in the tossing waves of contradiction and impossibility; but still his head would come up into the air and he would get a breath before he went down again. And with every fresh conflict, every fresh gleam of doubtful victory, the essential idea of the master looked more and more lovely. And he began to see the working of his doubts on the growth of his heart and soul—both widening and realizing his faith, and preventing it from becoming faith in an idea of God instead of in the living God—the God beyond as well as in the heart that thought and willed and imagined.

He had much time for reflection as he sat silent by the bedside of Leopold. Sometimes Helen would be sitting near, though generally when he arrived she went out for her walk, but never anything came to him he could utter to her. And she was one of those who learn little from other people. A change must pass upon her ere she could be rightly receptive. Some vapour or other that clouded her being must be driven to the winds first.

Mrs. Ramshorn had become at least reconciled to the frequent presence of the curate, partly from the testimony of Helen, partly from the witness of her own eyes to the quality of his ministrations. She was by no means one of the loveliest among women, yet she had a heart, and could appreciate some kinds of goodness which the arrogance of her relation to the church did not interfere to hide—for nothing is so deadening to the divine as an habitual dealing with the outsides of holy things—and she became half-friendly and quite courteous when she met the curate on the stair, and would now and then, when she thought of it, bring him a glass of wine as he sat by the bedside.

CHAPTER VIII.

AN EXAMINATION.

The acquaintance between the draper and the gate-keeper rapidly ripened into friendship. Very generally, as soon as he had shut his shop, Drew would walk to the park-gate to see Polwarth; and three times a week at least, the curate made one of the party. Much was then talked, more was thought, and I venture to say, more yet was understood.

One evening the curate went earlier than usual, and had tea with the Polwarths.

"Do you remember," he asked of his host, "once putting to me the question what our Lord came into this world for?"

"I do," answered Polwarth.

"And you remember I answered you wrong: I said it was to save the world."

"I do. But remember, I said *primarily*, for of course he did come to save the world."

"Yes, just so you put it. Well, I think I can answer the question correctly now, and in learning the true answer I have learned much. Did he not come first of all to do the will of his Father? Was not his Father first with him always and in everything—his fellow-men next—for they were his Father's?"

"I need not say it—you know that you are right. Jesus is tenfold a real person to you—is he not—since you discovered that truth?"

"I think so; I hope so. It does seem as if a grand simple reality had begun to dawn upon me out of the fog—the form as of a man pure and simple, *because* the eternal son of the Father."

"And now, may I not ask—are you able to accept the miracles, things in themselves so improbable?"

"If we suppose the question settled as to whether the man was what he said, then all that remains is to ask whether the works reported of him are consistent with what you can see of the character of the man."

"And to you they seem—?"

"Some consistent, others not. Concerning the latter I look for more light."

"Meantime let me ask you a question about them. What was the main object of miracles?"

"One thing at least I have learned, Mr. Polwarth and that is, not to answer any question of yours in a hurry," said Wingfold. "I will, if you please, take this one home with me, and hold the light to it."

"Do," said Polwarth, "and you will find it return you the light threefold.— One word more, ere Mr. Drew comes: do you still think of giving up your curacy?"

"I have almost forgotten I ever thought of such a thing. Whatever energies I may or may not have, I know one thing for certain, that I could not devote them to anything else I should think entirely worth doing. Indeed nothing else seems interesting enough—nothing to repay the labour, but the telling of my fellow-men about the one man who is the truth, and to know whom is the life. Even if there be no hereafter, I would live my time believing in a grand thing that ought to be true if it is not. No facts can take the place of truths, and if these be not truths, then is the loftiest part of our nature a waste. Let me hold by the better than the actual, and fall into nothingness off the same precipice with Jesus and John and Paul and a thousand more, who were lovely in their lives, and with their death make even the nothingness into which they have passed like the garden of the Lord. I will go further, Polwarth, and say, I would rather die for evermore believing as Jesus believed, than live for evermore believing as those that deny him. If there be no God, I feel assured that existence is and could be but a chaos of contradictions, whence can emerge nothing worthy to be called a truth, nothing worth living for.—No, I will not give up my curacy. I will teach that which IS good, even if there should be no God to make a fact of it, and I will spend my life on it, in the growing hope, which MAY become assurance, that there is indeed a perfect God, worthy of being the Father of Jesus Christ, and that it was BECAUSE they are true, that these things were lovely to me and to so many men and women, of whom some have died for them, and some would be yet ready to die."

"I thank my God to hear you say so. Nor will you stand still there," said Polwarth. "But here comes Mr. Drew!"

CHAPTER IX.

IMMORTALITY.

"How goes business?" said Polwarth, when the new-comer had seated himself.

"That is hardly a question I look for from you, sir," returned the draper, smiling all over his round face, which looked more than ever like a moon of superior intelligence. "For me, I am glad to leave it behind me in the shop."

"True business can never be left in any shop. It is a care, white or black, that sits behind every horseman."

"That is fact; and with me it has just taken a new shape," said Drew, "for I have come with quite a fresh difficulty. Since I saw you last, Mr. Polwarth, a strange and very uncomfortable doubt has rushed in upon me, and I find myself altogether unfit to tackle it. I have no weapons—not a single argument of the least weight. I wonder if it be a law of nature that no sooner shall a man get into a muddle with one thing, than a thousand other muddles shall come pouring in upon him, as if Muddle itself were going to swallow him up! Here am I just beginning to get a little start in honester ways, when up comes the ugly head of the said doubt, swelling itself more and more to look like a fact—namely, that after this world there is nothing for us—nothing at all to be had anyhow—that as we came so we go—into life, out of life—that, having been nothing before, we shall be nothing after! The flowers come back in the spring, and the corn in the autumn, but they ain't the same flowers or the same corn. They're just as different as the new generations of men."

"There's no pretence that we come back either. We only think we don't go into the ground, but away somewhere else."

"You can't prove that."

"No."

"And you don't know anything about it!"

"Not much—but enough, I think."

"Why, even those that profess to believe it, scoff at the idea of an apparition—a ghost!"

"That's the fault of the ghosts, I suspect—or their reporters. I don't care about them myself. I prefer the tale of one who, they say, rose again, and brought his body with him."

"Yes; but he was only one!"

"Except two or three whom, they say, he brought to life."

"Still there are but three or four."

"To tell you the truth, I do not care much to argue the point with you.—It is by no means a matter of the FIRST importance whether we live for ever or not."

"Mr. Polwarth!" exclaimed the draper in such astonishment mingled with horror, as proved he was not in immediate danger of becoming an advocate of the doctrine of extinction.

The gate-keeper smiled what, but for a peculiar expression of undefinable good in it, might have been called a knowing smile.

"Suppose a thing were in itself not worth having," he said, "would it be any great enhancement of it as a gift to add the assurance that the possession of it was eternal! Most people think it a fine thing to have a bit of land to call their own and leave to their children; but suppose a stinking and undrainable swamp, full of foul springs—what consolation would it be to the proprietor of that to know, while the world lasted, not a human being would once dispute its possession with any fortunate descendant holding it?"

The draper only stared, but his stare was a thorough one. The curate sat waiting, with both amusement and interest, for what would follow: he saw the direction in which the little man was driving.

"You astonish me!" said Mr. Drew, recovering his mental breath. "How can you compare God's gift to such a horrible thing! Where should we be without life?"

Rachel burst out laughing, and the curate could not help joining her.

"Mr. Drew," said Polwarth, half merrily, "are you going to help me drag my chain out of its weary length, or are you too much shocked at the doubtful condition of its links to touch them? I promise you the last shall be of bright gold."

"I beg your pardon," said the draper; "I might have known you didn't mean it."

"On the contrary, I mean everything I say and that literally. Perhaps I don't mean everything you fancy I mean.—Tell me then, would life be worth having on any and every possible condition?"

"Certainly not."

"You know some, I dare say, who would be glad to be rid of life such as it is, and such as they suppose it must continue?"

"I don't."

"I do."

"I have already understood that everybody clung to life."

"Most people do; everybody certainly does not: Job, for instance."

"They say that is but a poem."

"BUT a poem! EVEN a poem—a representation true not of this or that individual, but of the race! There ARE such persons as would gladly be rid of life, and in their condition all would feel the same. Somewhat similar is the state of those who profess unbelief in the existence of God: none of them expect, and few of them seem to wish to live for ever!—At least, so I am told."

"That is no wonder," said the draper; "—if they don't believe in God, I mean."

"Then there I have you! There you allow life to be not worth having, if on certain evil conditions."

"I admit it, then."

"And I repeat that to prove life endless is a matter of the FIRST importance. And I will go a little farther.—Does it follow that life is worth having because a man would like to have it for ever?"

"I should say so; who should be a better judge than the man himself?"

"Let us look at it a moment. Suppose—we will take a strong case—suppose a man whose whole delight is in cruelty, and who has such plentiful opportunity of indulging the passion that he finds it well with him—such a man would of course desire such a life to endure for ever: is such a life worth having? were it well that man should be immortally cruel?"

"Not for others."

"Still less, I say, for himself."

"In the judgment of others, doubtless; but to himself he would be happy."

"Call his horrible satisfaction happiness then, and leave aside the fact that in its own nature it is a horror, and not a bliss: a time must come, when, in the exercise of his delight, he shall have destroyed all life besides, and made himself alone with himself in an empty world: will he then find life worth having?"

"Then he ought to live for punishment."

"With that we have nothing to do now, but there you have given me an answer to my question, whether a man's judgment that his life is worth having, proves immortality a thing to be desired."

"I have. I understand now."

"It follows that there is something of prior importance to the possession of immortality:—what is that something?"

"I suppose that the immortality itself should be worth possessing."

"Yes; that the life should be such that it were well it should be endless.—And what then if it be not such?"

"The question then would be whether it could not be made such."

"You are right.—And wherein consists the essential inherent worthiness of a life as life?—The only perfect idea of life is—a unit, self-existent, and creative. That is God, the only one. But to this idea, in its kind, must every life, to be complete as life, correspond; and the human correspondence to self-existence is, that the man should round and complete himself by taking into himself that origin; by going back and in his own will adopting his origin, rooting therein afresh in the exercise of his own freedom and in all the energy of his own self-roused will; in other words—that the man say "I will be after the will of the creating *I*;" that he see and say with his whole being that to will the will of God in himself and for himself and concerning himself, is the highest possible condition of a man. Then has he completed his cycle by turning back upon his history, laying hold of his cause, and willing his own being in the will of the only I AM. This is the rounding, re-creating, unifying of the man. This is religion, and all that gathers not with this, scatters abroad."

"And then," said Drew, with some eagerness, "lawfully comes the question, 'Shall I, or shall I not live for ever?'"

"Pardon me; I think not," returned the little prophet. "I think rather we have done with it for ever. The man with life so in himself, will not dream of asking whether he shall live. It is only in the twilight of a half-life, holding in it at once much wherefore it should desire its own continuance, and much that renders it unworthy of continuance, that the doubtful desire of immortality can arise.—Do you remember"—here Polwarth turned to Wingfold—"my mentioning to you once a certain manuscript of strange interest—to me at least and Rachel—which a brother of mine left behind him?"

"I remember it perfectly," answered the curate."

"It seems so to mingle with all I ever think on this question, that I should much like, if you gentlemen would allow me, to read some extracts from it."

Nothing could have been heartier than the assurance of both the men that they could but be delighted to listen to anything he chose to give them.

"I must first tell you, however," said Polwarth, "merely to protect you from certain disturbing speculations, otherwise sure to present themselves, that my poor brother was mad, and that what I now read portions of seemed to him no play of the imagination, but a record of absolute fact. Some parts are stranger and less intelligible than others, but through it all there is abundance of intellectual movement, and what seems to me a wonderful keenness to perceive the movements and arrest the indications of an imagined consciousness."

As he spoke, the little man was opening a cabinet in which he kept his precious things. He brought from it a good-sized quarto volume, neatly bound in morocco, with gilt edges, which he seemed to handle not merely with respect but with tenderness.

The heading of the next chapter is my own, and does not belong to the manuscript.

CHAPTER X.

PASSAGES FROM THE AUTOBIOGRAPHY OF THE WANDERING JEW.

"'I have at length been ill, very ill, once more, and for many reasons foreign to the weightiest, which I had forgotten, I had hoped that I was going to die. But therein I am as usual deceived and disappointed. That I have been out of my mind I know, by having returned to the real knowledge of what I am. The conscious present has again fallen together and made a whole with the past, and that whole is my personal identity.

"'How I broke loose from the bonds of a madness, which, after so many and heavy years of uninterrupted sanity, had at length laid hold upon me, I will now relate.

"'I had, as I have said, been very ill—with some sort of fever that had found fit rooting in a brain overwearied, from not having been originally constructed to last so long. Whether it came not of an indwelling demon, or a legion of demons, I cannot tell—God knows. Surely I was as one possessed. I was mad, whether for years, or but for moments—who can tell? I cannot. Verily it seems for many years; but, knowing well the truth concerning the relations of time in him that dreameth and waketh from his dream, I place no confidence in the testimony of the impressions left upon my seeming memory. I can however trust it sufficiently as to the character of the illusions that then possessed me. I imagined myself an Englishman called Polwarth, of an ancient Cornish family. Indeed, I had in my imagination, as Polwarth, gone through the history, every day of it, with its sunrise and sunset, of more than half a lifetime. I had a brother who was deformed and a dwarf, and a daughter who was like him; and the only thing, throughout the madness, that approached a consciousness of my real being and history, was the impression that these things had come upon me because of a certain grievous wrong I had at one time committed, which wrong, however, I had quite forgotten— and could ill have imagined in its native hideousness.

"'But one morning, just as I woke, after a restless night filled with dreams, I was aware of a half-embodied shadow in my mind— whether thought or memory or imagination, I could not tell: and the strange thing was, that it darkly radiated from it the conviction that I must hold and identify it, or be for ever lost to myself. Therefore, with all the might of my will to retain the shadow, and all the energy of my recollection to recall that of which it was the vague shadow, I concentrated the whole power of my spiritual man upon the phantom thought, to fix and retain it.

"'Everyone knows what it is to hunt such a formless fact. Evanescent as a rainbow, its whole appearance, from the first, is that of a thing in the act of vanishing. It is a thing that was known, but, from the moment consciousness turned its lantern upon it, began to become invisible. For a time, during the close pursuit that follows, it seems only to be turning corner after corner to evade the mind's eye, but behind every corner it leaves a portion of itself; until at length, although when finally cannot be told, it is gone so utterly that the mind remains aghast in the perplexity of the doubt whether ever there was a thought there at all.

"'Throughout my delusion of an English existence, I had been tormented in my wakings with such thought-phantoms, and ever had I followed them, as an idle man may follow a flitting marsh-fire. Indeed, I had grown so much interested in the phenomenon and its possible indications that I had invented various theories to account for them, some of which seemed to myself original and ingenious, while the common idea that they are vague reminiscences of a former state of being, I had again and again examined, and as often entirely rejected, as in no way tenable or verisimilar.

"'But upon the morning to which I have referred, I succeeded, for the first time, in fixing, capturing, identifying the haunting, fluttering thing. That moment the bonds of my madness were broken. My past returned upon me. I had but to think in any direction, and every occurrence, with time and place and all its circumstance, rose again before me. The awful fact of my own being once more stood bare—awful always—tenfold more awful after such a period of blissful oblivion thereof: I was, I had been, I am now, as I write, the man so mysterious in crime, so unlike all other men in his punishment, known by various names in various lands—here in England as the Wandering Jew. Ahasuerus was himself again, alas!—himself and no other. Wife, daughter, brother vanished, and returned only in dreams. I was and remain the wanderer, the undying, the repentant, the unforgiven. O heart! O weary feet! O eyes that have seen and never more shall see, until they see once and are blinded for ever! Back upon my soul rushes the memory of my deed, like a storm of hail mingled with fire, flashing through every old dry channel, that it throbs and writhes anew, scorched at once and torn with the poisonous burning."

CHAPTER XI.

THE WANDERING JEW.

"'It was a fair summer-morning in holy Jerusalem, and I sat and wrought at my trade, for I sewed a pair of sandals for the feet of the high priest Caiaphas. And I wrought diligently, for it behoved me to cease an hour ere set of sun, for it was the day of preparation for the eating of the Passover.

"'Now all that night there had been a going to and fro in the city, for the chief priests and their followers had at length laid hands upon him that was called Jesus, whom some believed to be the Messiah, and others, with my fool-self amongst them, an arch-impostor and blasphemer. For I was of the house of Caiaphas, and heartily did desire that the man my lord declared a deceiver of the people, should meet with the just reward of his doings. Thus I sat and worked, and thought and rejoiced; and the morning passed and the noon came.

"'It was a day of sultry summer, and the street burned beneath the sun, and I sat in the shadow and looked out upon the glare; and ever I wrought at the sandals of my lord, with many fine stitches, in cunning workmanship. All had been for some time very still, when suddenly I thought I heard a far-off tumult. And soon came the idle children, who ever run first that they be not swallowed up of the crowd; and they ran and looked behind as they ran. And after them came the crowd, crying and shouting, and swaying hither and thither; and in the midst of it arose the one arm of a cross, beneath the weight of which that same Jesus bent so low that I saw him not. Truly, said I, he hath not seldom borne heavier burdens in the workshop of his father the Galilean, but now his sins and his idleness have found him, and taken from him his vigour; for he that despiseth the law shall perish, while they that wait upon the Lord shall renew their strength. For I was wroth with the man who taught the people to despise the great ones that administered the law, and give honour to the small ones who only kept it. Besides, he had driven my father's brother from the court of the Gentiles with a whip, which truly hurt him not outwardly, but stung him to the soul; and yet that very temple which he pretended thus to honour, he had threatened to destroy and build again in three days! Such were the thoughts of my heart; and when I learned from the boys that it was in truth Jesus of Nazareth who passed on his way to Calvary to be crucified, my heart leaped within me at the thought that the law had at length overtaken the malefactor. I laid down the sandal and my awl, and rose and went forth and stood in the front of my shop. And Jesus drew nigh, and as he passed, lo, the end of the cross dragged upon the street. And one in the crowd came behind, and lifted it up and pushed therewith, so that Jesus staggered and had nigh fallen. Then would be fain have rested the arm of the cross on the stone by which I was wont to go up into my shop from the street. But I cried out, and drove him thence, saying scornfully, "Go on Jesus; go on. Truly thou restest not on stone of mine!" Then turned he his eyes upon me, and said, "I go indeed, but thou goest not;" and therewith he rose again under the weight of the cross, and staggered on,

"'And I followed in the crowd to Calvary.'"

Here the reader paused and said,

"I can give you but a few passages now. You see it is a large manuscript. I will therefore choose some of those that bear upon the subject of which we have been talking. A detailed account of the crucifixion follows here, which I could not bring myself to read aloud. The eclipse is in it, and the earthquake, and the white faces of the risen dead gleaming through the darkness about the cross. It ends thus:

"'And all the time, I stood not far from the foot of the cross, nor dared go nearer, for around it were his mother and they that were with her, and my heart was sore for her also. And I would have withdrawn my foot from the place where I stood, and gone home to weep, but something, I know not what, held me there as it were rooted to the ground. At length the end was drawing near. He opened his mouth and spake to his mother and the disciple who stood by her, but truly I know not what he said, for as his eyes turned from them, they looked upon me, and my heart died within me. He said nought, but his eyes had that in them that would have slain me with sorrow, had not death, although I knew it not, already shrunk from my presence, daring no more come nigh such a malefactor.—Oh Death, how gladly would I build thee a temple, set thee in a lofty place, and worship thee with the sacrifice of vultures on a fire of dead men's bones, wouldst thou but hear my cry!—But I rave again in my folly! God forgive me. All the days of my appointed time will I wait until my change come.—With that look—a well of everlasting tears in my throbbing brain—my feet were unrooted, and I fled.'"

Here the reader paused again, and turned over many leaves.

"'And ever as I passed at night through the lands, when I came to a cross by the wayside, thereon would I climb, and, winding my arms about its arms and my feet about its stem, would there hang in the darkness or the moon, in rain or hail, in wind or snow or frost, until my sinews gave way, and my body dropped, and I knew no more until I found myself lying at its foot in the morning. For, ever in such case, I lay without sense until again the sun shone upon me.

"'... And if ever the memory of that look passed from me, then, straightway I began to long for death, and so longed until the memory and the power of the look came again, and with the sorrow in my soul came the patience to live. And truly, although I speak of forgetting and remembering, such motions of my spirit in me were not as those of another man; in me they are not measured by the scale of men's lives; they are not of years, but of centuries; for the seconds of my life are ticked by a clock whose pendulum swings through an arc of motionless stars.

"'... Once I had a vision of Death. Methinks it must have been a precursive vapour of the madness that afterwards infolded me, for I know well that there is not one called Death, that he is but a word needful to the weakness of human thought and the poverty of human speech; that he is a no-being, and but a change from that which is.—I had a vision of Death, I say. And it was on this wise:

"'I was walking over a wide plain of sand, like Egypt, so that ever and anon I looked around me to see if nowhere, from the base of the horizon, the pyramids cut their triangle out of the blue night of heaven; but I saw none. The stars came down and sparkled on the dry sands, and all was waste, and wide desolation. The air also was still as the air of a walled-up tomb, where there are but dry bones, and not even the wind of an evil vapour that rises from decay. And through the dead air came ever the low moaning of a distant sea, towards which my feet did bear me. I had been journeying thus for years, and in their lapse it had grown but a little louder.—Suddenly I was aware that I was not alone. A dim figure strode beside me, vague, but certain of presence. And I feared him not, seeing that which men fear the most was itself that which by me was the most desired. So I stood and turned and would have spoken. But the shade that seemed not a shadow, went on and regarded me not. Then I also turned again towards the moaning of the sea and went on. And lo! the shade which had gone before until it seemed but as a vapour among the stars, was again by my side walking. And I said, and stood not, but walked on: Thou shade that art not a shadow, seeing there shineth no sun or moon, and the stars are many, and the one slayeth the shadow of the other, what art thou, and wherefore goest thou by my side? Think not to make me afraid, for I fear nothing in the universe but that which I love the best.—I spake of the eyes of the Lord Jesus.—Then the shade that seemed no shadow answered me and spake and said: Little knowest thou what I am, seeing the very thing thou sayest I am not, that I am, and nought else, and there is no other but me. I am Shadow, the shadow, the only shadow—none such as those from which the light hideth in terror, yet like them, for life hideth from me and turneth away, yet if life were not, neither were I, for I am nothing; and yet again, as soon as anything is, there am I, and needed no maker, but came of myself, for I am Death.—Ha! Death! I cried, and would have cast myself before him with outstretched arms of worshipful entreaty; but lo, there was a shadow upon the belt of Orion, and no shadow by my side! and I sighed, and walked on towards the ever moaning sea. Then again the shadow was by my side. And again I spake and said: Thou thing of flitting and return, I despise thee, for thou wilt not abide the conflict. And I would have cast myself upon him and wrestled with him there, for defeat and not for victory. But I could not lay hold upon him. Thou art a powerless nothing, I cried; I will not even defy thee.—Thou wouldst provoke me, said the shadow; but it availeth not. I cannot be provoked. Truly, I am but a shadow, yet know I my own worth, for I am the Shadow of the Almighty, and where he is, there am I—Thou art nothing, I said.—Nay, nay, I am not Nothing. Thou, nor any man—God only knoweth what that word meaneth. I am but the shadow of Nothing, and when THOU sayest NOTHING, thou meanest only me; but what God meaneth when he sayeth NOTHING—the nothing without him, that nothing which is no shadow but the very substance of Unbeing—no created soul can know.—Then art thou not Death? I asked.—I am what thou thinkest of when thou sayest Death, he answered, but I am not Death.—Alas, then! why comest thou to me in the desert places, for I did think thou wast Death indeed, and couldst take me unto thee so that I should be no more.—That is what death cannot do for thee, said the shadow; none but he that created thee can cause that thou shouldst be no more. Thou art until he will that thou be not. I have heard it said amongst the wise that, hard as it is to create, it is harder still to uncreate. Truly I cannot tell. But wouldst thou be uncreated by the hand of Death? Wouldst thou have thy no-being the gift of a shadow?—Then I thought of the eyes of the Lord Jesus, and the look he cast upon me, and I said, No: I would not be carried away of Death. I would be fulfilled of Life, and stand before God for ever. Then once again the belt of Orion grew dim, and I saw the shadow no more. And yet did I long for Death, for I thought he might bring me to those eyes, and the pardon that lay in them.

"'But again, as the years went on, and each brought less hope than that before it, I forgot the look the Lord had cast upon me, and in the weariness of the life that was mortal and yet would not cease, in the longing after the natural end of that which against nature endured, I began to long even for the end of being itself. And in a city of the Germans, I found certain men of my own nation who said unto me: Fear not, Ahasuerus; there is no life beyond the grave. Live on until thy end come, and cease thy complaints. Who is there among us who would not gladly take upon him thy judgment, and live until he was weary of living?—Yea, but to live after thou art weary? I said. But they heeded me not, answering me and saying: Search thou the Scriptures, even the Book of the Law, and see if thou find there one leaf of this gourd of a faith that hath sprung up in a night. Verily, this immortality is but a flash in the brain of men that would rise above their fate. Sayeth Moses, or sayeth Job, or sayeth David or Daniel a word of the matter? And I listened unto them, and became of their mind. But therewithal the longing after death returned with tenfold force and I rose up and girt my garment about me, and went forth once more to search for him whom I now took for the porter of the gate of eternal silence and unfelt repose. And I said unto myself as I walked: What in the old days was sweeter when I was weary with my labour at making of shoes, than to find myself dropping into the death of sleep! how much sweeter then must it not be to sink into the sleepiest of sleeps, the father-sleep, the mother-bosomed death of nothingness and unawaking rest! Then shall all this endless whir of the wheels of thought and desire be over; then welcome the night whose darkness doth not seethe, and which no morning shall ever stir!

"'And wherever armies were drawing nigh, each to the other, and the day of battle was near, thither I flew in hot haste, that I might be first upon the field, and ready to welcome hottest peril. I fought not, for I would not slay those that counted it not the good thing to be slain, as I counted it. But had the armies been of men that loved death like me, how had I raged among them then, even as the angel Azrael to give them their sore-desired rest! for I loved and hated not my kind, and would diligently have mown them down out of the stinging air of life into the soft balm of the sepulchre. But what they sought not, and I therefore would not give, that searched I after the more eagerly for myself. And my sight grew so keen that, when yet no bigger than a mote in the sunbeam, I could always descry the vulture-scout, hanging aloft over the field of destiny. Then would I hasten on and on, until a swoop would have brought him straight on my head.

"'And with that a troop of horsemen, horses and men mad with living fear, came with a level rush towards the spot where I sat, faint with woe. And I sprang up, and bounded to meet them, throwing my arms aloft and shouting, as one who would turn a herd. And like a wave of the rising tide before a swift wind, a wave that sweeps on and breaks not, they came hard-buffeting over my head. Ah! that was a torrent indeed!—a thunderous succession of solid billows, alive, hurled along by the hurricane-fear in the heart of them! For one moment only I felt and knew what I lay beneath, and then for a time there was nothing.—I woke in silence, and thought I was dying, that I had all but passed across the invisible line between, and in a moment there would be for evermore nothing and nothing. Then followed again an empty space as it seemed. And now I am dead and gone, I said, and shall wander no more. And with that came the agony of hell, for, lo, still *I* THOUGHT! And I said to myself, Alas! O God! for, notwithstanding I no more see or hear or taste or smell or touch, and my body hath dropped from me, still am I Ahasuerus, the Wanderer, and must go on and on and on, blind and deaf, through the unutterable wastes that know not the senses of man—nevermore to find rest! Alas! death is not death, seeing he slayeth but the leathern bottle, and spilleth not the wine of life upon the earth. Alas! alas! for I cannot die! And with that a finger twitched, and I shouted aloud for joy: I was yet in the body! And I sprang to my feet jubilant, and, lame and bruised and broken-armed, tottered away after Death, who yet might hold the secret of eternal repose. I was alive, but yet there was hope, for Death was yet before me! I was alive, but I had not died, and who could tell but I might yet find the lovely night that hath neither clouds nor stars! I had not passed into the land of the dead and found myself yet living! The wise men of my nation in the city of the Almains might yet be wise! And for an hour I rejoiced, and was glad greatly.'"

CHAPTER XII.

THE WANDERING JEW.

"It was midnight, and sultry as hell. All day not a breath had stirred. The country through which I passed was level as the sea that had once flowed above it. My heart had almost ceased to beat, and I was weary as the man who is too weary to sleep outright, and labours in his dreams. I slumbered and yet walked on. My blood flowed scarce faster than the sluggish water in the many canals I crossed on my weary way. And ever I thought to meet the shadow that was and was not death. But this was no dream. Just on the stroke of midnight, I came to the gate of a large city, and the watchers let me pass. Through many an ancient and lofty street I wandered, like a ghost in a dream, knowing no one, and caring not for myself, and at length reached an open space where stood a great church, the cross upon whose spire seemed bejewelled with the stars upon which it dwelt. And in my soul I said, O Lord Jesus! and went up to the base of the tower, and found the door thereof open to my hand. Then with my staff I ascended the winding stairs, until I reached the open sky. And the stairs went still winding, on and on, up towards the stars. And with my staff I ascended, and arose into the sky, until I stood at the foot of the cross of stone.

"'Ay me! how the centuries without haste, without rest, had glided along since I stood by the cross of dishonour and pain! And God had not grown weary of his life yet, but I had grown so weary in my very bones that weariness was my element, and I had ceased almost to note it. And now, high-uplifted in honour and worship over every populous city, stood the cross among the stars! I scrambled up the pinnacles, and up on the carven stem of the cross, for my sinews were as steel, and my muscles had dried and hardened until they were as those of the tiger or the great serpent. So I climbed, and lifted up myself until I reached the great arms of the cross, and over them I flung my arms, as was my wont, and entwined the stem with my legs, and there hung, three hundred feet above the roofs of the houses. And as I hung the moon rose and cast the shadow of me Ahasuerus upon the cross, up against the Pleiades. And as if dull Nature were offended thereat, nor understood the offering of my poor sacrifice, the clouds began to gather, like the vultures—no one could have told whence. From all sides around they rose, and the moon was blotted out, and they gathered and rose until they met right over the cross. And when they closed, then the lightning brake forth, and the thunder with it, and it flashed and thundered above and around and beneath me, so that I could not tell which voice belonged to which arrow, for all were mingled in one great confusion and uproar. And the people in the houses below heard the sound of the thunder, and they looked from their windows, and they saw the storm raving and flashing about the spire, which stood the heart of the agony, and they saw something hang there, even upon its cross, in the form of a man, and they came from their houses, and the whole space beneath was filled with people, who stood gazing up at the marvel. A MIRACLE! A MIRACLE! they cried; and truly it was no miracle— it was only me Ahasuerus, the wanderer taking thought concerning his crime against the crucified. Then came a great light all about me, such light for shining as I had never before beheld, and indeed I saw it not all with my eyes, but the greater part with my soul, which surely is the light of the eyes themselves. And I said to myself, Doubtless the Lord is at hand, and he cometh to me as late to the blessed Saul of Tarsus, who was NOT the chief of sinners, but I—Ahasuerus, the accursed. And the thunder burst like the bursting of a world in the furnace of the sun; and whether it was that the lightning struck me, or that I dropped, as was my custom, outwearied from the cross, I know not, but thereafter I lay at its foot among the pinnacles, and when the people looked again, the miracle was over, and they returned to their houses and slept. And the next day, when I sought the comfort of the bath, I found upon my side the figure of a cross, and the form of a man hanging thereupon as I had hung, depainted in a dark colour as of lead plain upon the flesh of my side over my heart. Here was a miracle indeed! but verily I knew not whether therefrom to gather comfort or despair.

"'And it was night as I went into a village among the mountains, through the desert places of which I had all that day been wandering. And never before had my condition seemed to me so hopeless. There was not one left upon the earth who had ever seen me knowing me, and although there went a tale of such a man as I, yet faith had so far vanished from the earth that for a thing to be marvellous, however just, was sufficient reason wherefore no man, to be counted wise, should believe the same. For the last fifty years I had found not one that would receive my testimony. For when I told them the truth concerning myself, saying as I now say, and knowing the thing for true—that I was Ahasuerus whom the Word had banished from his home in the regions governed of Death, shutting against him the door of the tomb that he should not go in, every man said I was mad, and would hold with me no manner of communication, more than if I had been possessed with a legion of swine-loving demons. Therefore was I cold at heart, and lonely to the very root of my being. And thus it was with me that midnight as I entered the village among the mountains.—Now all therein slept, so even that not a dog barked at the sound of my footsteps. But suddenly, and my soul yet quivers with dismay at the remembrance, a yell of horror tore its way from the throat of every sleeper at once, and shot into every cranny of the many-folded mountains, that my soul knocked shaking against the sides of my body, and I also shrieked aloud with the keen terror of the cry. For surely there was no sleeper there, man, woman, or child, who yelled not aloud in an agony of fear. And I knew that it could only be because of the unseen presence in their street of the outcast, the homeless, the loveless, the wanderer for ever, who had refused a stone to his maker whereon to rest his cross. Truly I know not whence else could have come that cry. And I looked to see that all the inhabitants of the village should rush out upon me, and go for to slay the unslayable in their agony. But the cry passed, and after the cry came again the stillness. And for very dread lest yet another such cry should enter my ears, and turn my heart to a jelly, I did hasten my steps to leave the dwellings of the children of the world, and pass out upon the pathless hills again. But as I turned and would have departed, the door of a house opened over against where I stood; and as it opened, lo! a sharp gust of wind from the mountains swept along the street, and out into the wind came running a girl, clothed only in the garment of the night. And the wind blew upon her, and by the light of the moon I saw that her hands and her feet were rough and brown, as of one that knew labour and hardship, but yet her body was dainty and fair, and moulded in loveliness. Her hair blew around her like a rain cloud, so that it almost blinded her, and truly she had much ado to clear it from her face, as a half-drowned man would clear from his face the waters whence he hath been lifted; and like two stars of light from amidst the cloud gazed forth the eyes of the girl. And she looked upon me with the courage of a child, and she said unto me, Stranger, knowest thou wherefore was that cry? Was it thou who did so cry in our street in the night? And I answered her and said, Verily not I, maiden, but I too heard the cry, and it shook my soul within me.—What seemed it unto thee like, she asked, for truly I slept, and know only the terror thereof and not the sound? And I said, It seemed unto me that every soul in the village cried out at once in some dream of horror.—I cried not out, she said; for I slept and dreamed, and my dream was such that I know verily I cried not out. And the maiden was lovely in her innocence. And I said: And was thy dream such, maiden, that thou wouldst not refuse but wouldst tell it to an old man like me? And with that the wind came down from the mountain like a torrent of wolves, and it laid hold upon me and swept me from the village, and I fled before it, and could not stay my steps until I got me into the covert of a hollow rock.

"'And scarce had I turned in thither when, lo! thither came the maiden also, flying in my footsteps, and driven of the self-same mighty wind. And I turned in pity and said, Fear not, my child. Here is but an old man with a sore and withered heart, and he will not harm thee.—I fear thee not, she answered, else would I not have followed thee.—Thou didst not follow me of thine own inclining, I said, but the wind that came from the mountains and swept me before it, did bear thee after me.—Truly I know of no wind, she said, but the wind of my own following of thee. Wherefore didst thou flee from me?—Nay! but wherefore didst thou follow me, maiden?—That I might tell thee my dream to the which thou didst desire to hearken. For, lo! as I slept I dreamed that a man came unto me and said, Behold, I am the unresting and undying one, and my burden is greater than I can bear, for Death who befriendeth all is my enemy, and will not look upon me in peace. And with that came the cry, and I awoke, and ran out to see whence came the cry, and found thee alone in the street. And as God liveth, such as was the man in my dream, such art thou in my waking sight.—Not the less must I ask thee again, I said, wherefore didst thou follow me?—That I may comfort thee, she answered.—And how thinkest thou to comfort one whom God hath forsaken?—That cannot be, she said, seeing that in a vision of the night he sent thee unto me, and so now hath sent me unto thee. Therefore will I go with thee, and minister unto thee.—Bethink thee well what thou doest, I said; and before thou art fully resolved, sit thee down by me in this cave, that I may tell thee my tale. And straightway she sat down, and I told her all. And ere I had finished the sun had risen.—Then art thou now alone, said the maiden, and hast no one to love thee?—No one, I answered, man, woman, or child.—Then will I go with thee, for I know neither father nor mother, and no one hath power over me, for I keep goats on the mountains for wages, and if thou wilt but give me bread to eat I will serve thee. And a great love arose in my heart to the maiden. And I left her in the cave, and went to the nearest city, and returned thence with garments and victuals. And I loved the maiden greatly. And although my age was then marvellous being over and above a thousand and seven hundred years, yet found she my person neither pitiful nor uncomely, for I was still in body even such as when the Lord Jesus spake the word of my doom. And the damsel loved me, and was mine. And she was as the apple of mine eye. And the world was no more unto me as a desert, but it blossomed as the rose of Sharon. And although I knew every city upon it, and every highway and navigable sea, yet did all become to me fresh and new because of the joy which the damsel had in beholding its kingdoms and the glories thereof.

"And it came to pass that my heart grew proud within me, and I said to myself that I was all-superior to other men, for Death could not touch me; that I was a marvel upon the face of the world; and in this yet more above all men that had ever lived, that at such an age as mine I could yet gain the love, yea, the absolute devotion, of such an one as my wife, who never wearied of my company and conversation. So I took to me even the free grace of love as my merit unto pride, and laid it not to the great gift of God and the tenderness of the heart of my beloved. Like Satan in Heaven I was uplifted in the strength and worthiness and honour of my demon-self, and my pride went not forth in thanks, for I gloried not in my God, but in Ahasuerus. Then the thought smote me like an arrow of lightning: She will die, and thou shalt live—live—live—and as he hath delayed, so will he yet delay his coming. And as Satan from the seventh heaven, I fell prone.

"'Then my spirit began again to revive within me, and I said, Lo! I have yet many years of her love ere she dieth, and when she is gone, I shall yet have the memory of my beloved to be with me, and cheer me, and bear me up, for I may never again despise that which she hath loved as she hath loved me. And yet again a thought smote me, and it was as an arrow of the lightning, and its barb was the truth: But she will grow old, it said, and will wither before thy face, and be as the waning moon in the heavens. And my heart cried out in an agony. But my will sought to comfort my heart, and said, Cry not out, for, in spite of old age as in spite of death, I will love her still. Then something began to writhe within me, and to hiss out words that gathered themselves unto this purpose: But she will grow unlovely, and wrinkled, and dark of hue, and the shape of her body will vanish, and her form be unformed, and her eyes will grow small and dim, and creep back into her head, and her hair will fall from her, and she shall be as the unsightly figure of Death with a skin drawn over his unseemly bones; and the damsel of thy love, with the round limbs and the flying hair, and the clear eyes out of which looketh a soul clear as they, will be nowhere—nowhere, for evermore, for thou wilt not be able to believe that she it is who standeth before thee: how will it be with thee then? And what mercy is his who hath sent thee a growing loss in the company of this woman? Thereupon I rose in the strength of my agony and went forth. And I said nothing unto my wife, but strode to the foot of the great mountain, whose entrails were all aglow, and on whose sides grew the palm and the tree-bread and the nut of milk. And I climbed the mountain, nor once looked behind me, but climbed to the top. And there for one moment I stood in the stock-dullness of despair. And beneath me was the great fiery gulf, outstretched like a red lake skinned over with black ice, through the cracks wherein shone the blinding fire. Every moment here and there a great liquid bubbling would break through the crust, and make a wallowing heap upon the flat, then sink again, leaving an open red well-pool of fire whence the rays shot up like flame, although flame there was none. It lay like the back of some huge animal upheaved out of hell, which was wounded and bled fire.—Now, in the last year of my long sojourn, life had again, because of the woman that loved me, become precious unto me, and more than once had I laughed as I caught myself starting back from some danger in a crowded street, for the thing was new to me, so utterly had the care of my life fallen into disuse with me. But now again in my misery I thought no more of danger, but went stalking and sliding down the sindery slope of the huge fire-cup, and out upon the lake of molten earth—molten as when first it shot from the womb of the sun, of whose ardour, through all the millions of years, it had not yet cooled. And as once St. Peter on the stormy water to find the Lord of Life, so walked I on the still lake of fire, caring neither for life nor death. For my heart was withered to the roots by the thought of the decay of her whom I had loved; for would not then her very presence every hour be causing me to forget the beauty that had once made me glad?—I had walked some ten furlongs, and passed the middle of the lake, when suddenly I bethought me that she would marvel whither I had gone, and set out to seek me, and something might befall her, and I should lose my rose ere its leaves had begun to drop. And I turned and strode again in haste across the floor of black heat, broken and seamed with red light. And lo! as I neared the midst of the lake, a form came towards me, walking in the very footsteps I had left behind me, nor had I to look again to know the gracious motion of my beloved. And the black ice broke at her foot, and the fire shone up on her face, and it was lovely as an angel of God, and the glow of her love outshone the glow of the nether fire. And I called not to stay her foot, for I judged that the sooner she was with me, the sooner would she be in safety, for I knew how to walk thereon better than she. And my heart sang a song within me in praise of the love of woman, but I thought only of the love of my woman to me, whom the fires of hell could not hold back from him who was worthy of her love; and my heart sent the song up to my lips; but, as the first word arose, sure itself a red bubble from the pit of glowing hell, the black crust burst up between us, and a great hillock of seething, slow-spouting, slow-falling, mad red fire arose. For a moment or two the molten mound bubbled and wallowed, then sank—and I saw not my wife. Headlong I plunged into the fiery pool at my feet, and the clinging torture hurt me not, and I caught her in my arms, and rose to the surface, and crept forth, and shook the fire from mine eyes, and lo! I held to my bosom but as the fragment of a cinder of the furnace. And I laughed aloud in my madness, and the devils below heard me, and laughed yet again. O Age! O Decay! I cried, see how I triumph over thee: what canst thou do to this? And I flung the cinder from me into the pool, and plunged again into the grinning fire. But it cast me out seven times, and the seventh time I turned from it, and rushed out of the valley of burning, and threw myself on the mountain-side in the moonlight, and awoke mad.

"'And what I had then said in despair, I said yet again in thankfulness. O Age! O Decay! I cried, what canst thou now do to destroy the image of her which I bear nested in my heart of hearts? That at least is safe, I thank God. And from that hour I never more believed that I should die when at length my body dropped from me. If the thought came, it came as a fear, and not as a thing concerning which a man may say I would or I would not. For a mighty hope had arisen within me that yet I should stand forgiven in the eyes of him that was crucified, and that in token of his forgiveness he would grant me to look again, but in peace, upon the face of her that had loved me. O mighty Love, who can tell to what heights of perfection thou mayest yet rise in the bosom of the meanest who followeth the Crucified!'"

CHAPTER XIII.

REMARKS.

Polwarth closed the manuscript, and for a time no one spoke.

"The man who wrote that book," said Wingfold, "could not have been all out of his right mind."

"I must confess to you," returned Polwarth, "that I have chosen some of the more striking passages—only some of them however. One thing is pretty clear—that, granted the imagined conditions, within that circle the writer is sane enough—as sane at least as the Wandering Jew himself could well have been."

"Could you trust me with the manuscript, Mr. Polwarth?" said the curate.

"Willingly," said Polwarth, handing it to him.

"And I may carry it home with me?"

"Certainly."

"I shall take right good care of it. Are there any further memorials of struggle with unbelief?"

"Yes, there are some; for mood and not conviction must, in such a mind, often rule the hour. Sometimes he can believe; sometimes he cannot: he is a great man indeed who can always rise above his own moods! There is one passage I specially remember in which after his own fashion he treats of the existence of a God. You will know the one I mean when you come to it."

"It is indeed a treasure!" said the curate, taking the book and regarding it with prizing eyes. In his heart he was thinking of Leopold and Helen. And while he thus regarded the book, he was himself regarded of the gray luminous eyes of Rachel. What shone from those eyes may have been her delight at hearing him so speak of the book, for the hand that wrote it was that of her father; but there was a lingering in her gaze, not unmixed with questioning, and a certain indescribable liquidity in its light, reminding one of the stars as seen through a clear air from which the dew settles thick, that might have made a mother anxious. Alas for many a woman whose outward form is ungainly— she has a full round heart under the twisted ribs!

Why then should I say alas? Were it better that the heart were like the shape? or are such as Rachel forgotten before the God of the sparrows? No, surely; but he who most distinctly believes that from before the face of God every sorrow shall vanish, that they that sow in tears shall reap in joy, that death is but a mist that for a season swathes the spirit, and that, ever as the self-seeking vanishes from love, it groweth more full of delight—even he who with all his heart believes this, may be mournful over the aching of another heart while yet it lasts; and he who looks for his own death as his resurrection, may yet be sorrowful at every pale sunset that reminds him of the departure of the beloved before him.

The curate rose and took his departure, but the light of the gaze that had rested upon him lingered yet on the countenance of Rachel, and a sad half-smile hung over the motions of the baby-like fingers that knitted so busily.

The draper followed the curate, and Polwarth went up to his own room: he never could keep off his knees for long together. And as soon as she was alone, Rachel's hands dropped on her lap, her eyes closed, and her lips moved with solemn sweet motions. If there was a hearing ear open to that little house, oh surely those two were blessed! If not, then kind death was yet for a certainty drawing nigh—only, what if in deep hell there should be yet a deeper hell? And until slow Death arrive, what loving heart can bear the load that stupid Chance or still more stupid Fate has heaped upon it? Yet had I rather be crushed beneath the weight of mine, and die with my friends in the moaning of eternal farewells, than live like George Bascombe to carry lightly his little bag of content. A cursed confusion indeed is the universe, if it be no creation, but the helpless unhelpable thing such men would have us believe it—the hotbed mother of the children of an iron Necessity. Can any damnation be worse than this damning into an existence from which there is no refuge but a doubtful death?

Drew overtook Wingfold, and they walked together into Glaston.

"Wasn't that splendid?" said the draper.

"Hath not God chosen the weak things of the world to confound the mighty?" returned the curate. "Even through the play of a mad-man's imagination, the spirit of a sound mind may speak. Did you not find in it some stuff that would shape into answers to your questions?"

"I ought to have done so, I dare say," answered the draper, "but to tell the truth, I was so taken up with the wild story, and the style of the thing, and the little man's way of reading it, that I never thought of what I was full of when I came."

They parted at the shop, and the curate went on.

CHAPTER XIV.

STRUGGLES.

He stopped at the Manor House, for it was only beginning to be late, to inquire after Leopold. Helen received him with her usual coldness—a manner which was in part assumed for self-protection, for in his presence she always felt rebuked, and which had the effect of a veil between them to hide from her much of the curate's character that might otherwise have been intelligible to her. Leopold, she said, was a little better, but Wingfold walked home thinking what a happy thing it would be if God were to take him away.

His interest in Helen deepened and deepened. He could not help admiring her strength of character even when he saw it spent for worse than nought; and her devotion to her brother was lovely, notwithstanding the stains of selfishness that spotted it. Her moral standard was indeed far from lofty, and as to her spiritual nature, that as yet appeared nowhere. And yet the growth in her was marvellous when he thought of what she had seemed before this trouble came. One evening as he left Leopold, he heard her singing, and stood on the stair to listen. And to listen was to marvel. For her voice, instead of being hard and dry, as when he heard it before, was, without any loss of elasticity, now liquid and mellifluous, and full of feeling. Its tones were borne along like the leaves on the wild west wind of Shelley's sonnet. And the longing of the curate to help her from that moment took a fresh departure, and grew and grew. But as the hours and days and weeks passed, and the longing found no outlet, it turned to an almost hopeless brooding upon the face and the form, yea the heart and soul of the woman he so fain would help, until ere long he loved her with the passion of a man mingled with the compassion of a prophet. He saw that something had to be done IN her—perhaps that some saving shock in the guise of ruin had to visit her; that some door had to be burst open, some roof blown away, some rock blasted, that light and air might have free course through her soul's house, without which that soul could never grow stately like the house it inhabited. Whatever might be destined to effect this, for the chance of rendering poorest and most servile aid, he would watch and did watch, in silence and self-restraint, lest he should be betrayed into any presumptuous word that might breathe frost instead of balm upon the buds of her delaying Spring. If he might but be allowed to minister when at length the sleeping soul should stir! If its waking glance—ah! if it might fall on him! As often as the thought intruded, his heart would give one delirious bound, then couch ashamed of its presumption. He would not, he dared not look in that direction. He accused himself of mingling earthly motives and feelings with the unselfish and true, and scorned himself because of it. And was not Bascombe already the favoured friend of her heart?

Yet how could it be of her heart? for what concern had hearts in a common unbelief? None; but there were the hearts—the man and the woman—notwithstanding, who might yet well be drawn together by the unknown divine which they also shared; and that Helen, whose foot seemed now to approach and now to shun the line betwixt the kingdom of this world and the kingdom of heaven, should retire with such a guide into the deserts of denial and chosen godlessness, was to Wingfold a thought of torture almost unendurable. The thought of its possibility, nay, probability—for were not such unfitnesses continually becoming facts?—threatened sometimes to upset the whole fabric of his faith, although reared in spite of theology, adverse philosophy, and the most honest and bewildering doubt. That such a thing should be possible seemed at those times to bear more against the existence of a God than all the other grounds of question together. Then a shudder would go to the very deeps of his heart, and he would lay himself silent before the presence for a time; or make haste into the solitudes—not where the sun shone and the water ran, but where the light was dim and the wind low in the pine woods. There, where the sombre green vaults were upheld by a hundred slender columns, and the far-receding aisles seemed to lead to the ancestral home of shadows, there, his own soul a shadow of grief and fear among the shades of the gloomy temple, he bowed his heart before the Eternal, gathered together all the might of his being, and groaned forth in deepest effort of a will that struggled to be: "Thy will be done, and not mine." Then would his spirit again walk erect, and carry its burden as a cross and not as a gravestone.

Sometimes he was sorely perplexed to think how the weakness, as he called it, had begun, and how it had grown upon him. He could not say it was his doing, and what had he ever been aware of in it against which he ought to have striven? Came not the whole thing of his nature, a nature that was not of his design, and was beyond him and his control—a nature that either sprung from a God, or grew out of an unconscious Fate? If from the latter, how was such as he to encounter and reduce to a constrained and self-rejecting reason a Self unreasonable, being an issue of the Unreasoning, which Self was yet greater than he, its vagaries the source of his intensest consciousness and brightest glimpses of the ideal and all-desirable. If on the other hand it was born of a God, then let that God look to it, for, sure, that which belonged to his nature could not be evil or of small account in the eyes of him who made him in his own image. But alas! that image had, no matter how, been so defaced, that the will of the man might even now be setting itself up against the will of the God! Did his love then spring from the God-will or the man-will? Must there not be some God-way of the thing, all right and nothing wrong?—But he could not compass it, and the marvel to himself was that all the time he was able to go on preaching, and that with some sense of honesty and joy in his work.

In this trouble more than ever Wingfold felt that if there was no God, his soul was but a thing of rags and patches out in the masterless pitiless storm and hail of a chaotic universe. Often would he rush into the dark, as it were, crying for God, and ever he would emerge therefrom with some tincture of the light, enough to keep him alive and send him to his work. And there, in her own seat, Sunday after Sunday, sat the woman whom he had seen ten times, and that for no hasty moments, during the week, by the bedside of her brother, yet to whom only now, in the open secrecy of the pulpit, did he dare utter the words of might he would so fain have poured direct into her suffering heart. And there, Sunday after Sunday, the face he loved bore witness to the trouble of the heart he loved yet more: that heart was not yet redeemed! oh, might it be granted him to set some little wind a blowing for its revival and hope! As often as he stood up to preach, his heart swelled with the message he bore—a message of no private interpretation, but for the healing of the nations, yet a message for her, and for the healing of every individual heart that would hear and take, and he spoke with the freedom and dignity of a prophet. But when he saw her afterwards, he scarcely dared let his eyes rest a moment on her face, would only pluck the flower of a glance flying, or steal it at such moments when he thought she would not see. She caught his glance however far oftener than he knew, and was sometimes aware of it without seeing it at all. And there was that in the curate's behaviour, in his absolute avoidance of self-assertion, or the least possible intrusion upon her mental privacy—in the wrapping of his garments around him as it were, that his presence might offend as little as might be, while at the same time he was full of simple direct ministration to her brother, without one side-glance that sought approval of her, which the nobility of the woman could not fail to note, and seek to understand.

It was altogether a time of great struggle with Wingfold. He seemed to be assailed in every direction, and to feel the strong house of life giving way in every part, and yet he held on—lived, which he thought was all, and, without knowing it, grew. Perhaps it may be this period that the following verses which I found among his papers belong: he could not himself tell me.—

Out of my door I run to do the thing
That calls upon me. Straight the wind of words
Whoops from mine ears the sounds of them that sing
About their work—My God! my Father-King.

I turn in haste to see thy blessed door,
But lo! a cloud of flies and bats and birds,
And stalking vapours, and vague monster herds,
Have risen and lighted, rushed and swollen between.

Ah me! the house of peace is there no more.
Was it a dream then? Walls, fireside, and floor,
And sweet obedience, loving, calm, and free,
Are vanished—gone as they had never been.

I labour groaning. Comes a sudden sheen!—
And I am kneeling at my Father's knee,
Sighing with joy, and hoping utterly.

CHAPTER XV.

THE LAWN.

Leopold had begun to cough, and the fever continued. Every afternoon came the red flush to his cheek, and the hard glitter into his eye. His talk was then excited, and mostly about his coming trial. To Helen it was terribly painful, and she confessed to herself that but for Wingfold she must have given way. Leopold insisted on seeing Mr. Hooker every time he called, and every time expressed the hope that he would not allow pity for his weak state to prevent him from applying the severe remedy of the law to his moral condition. But in truth it began to look doubtful whether disease would not run a race with law for his life, even if the latter should at once proceed to justify a claim. From the first Faber doubted if he would ever recover from the consequences of that exposure in the churchyard, and it soon became evident that his lungs were more than affected. His cough increased, and he began to lose what little flesh he had.

One day Faber expressed his conviction to Wingfold that he was fighting the disease at the great disadvantage of having an unknown enemy to contend with.

"The fellow is unhappy," he said, "and if that lasts another month, I shall throw up the sponge. He has a good deal of vitality, but it is yielding, and by that time he will be in a galloping consumption."

"You must do your best for him," said Wingfold, but in his heart he wished, with an honest affection, that he might not succeed.

Leopold, however, seemed to have no idea of his condition, and the curate wondered what he would think or do were he to learn that he was dying. Would he insist on completing his confession, and urging on a trial? He had himself told him all that had passed with the magistrate, and how things now were as he understood them, but it was plain that he had begun to be uneasy about the affair, and was doubtful at times whether all was as it seemed. The curate was not deceived. He had been present during a visit from Mr. Hooker, and nothing could be plainer than the impression out of which the good man spoke. Nor could he fail to suspect the cunning kindness of George Bascombe in the affair. But he did not judge that he had now the least call to interfere. The poor boy had done as much as lay either in or out of him in the direction of duty, and was daily becoming more and more unfit either to originate or carry out a further course of action. If he was in himself capable of anything more, he was, in his present state of weakness, utterly unable to cope with the will of those around him.

Faber would have had him leave the country for some southern climate, but he would not hear of it, and Helen, knowing to what extremities it might drive him, would not insist. Nor, indeed, was he now in a condition to be moved. Also the weather had grown colder, and he was sensitive to atmospheric changes as any creature of the elements.

But after a fortnight, when it was now the middle of the autumn, it grew quite warm again, and he revived and made such progress that he was able to be carried into the garden every day. There he sat in a chair on the lawn, with his feet on a sheepskin, and a fur cloak about him. And for all the pain at his heart, for all the misery in which no one could share, for all the pangs of a helpless jealousy, checked only by a gnawing remorse, both of which took refuge in the thought of following through the spheres until he found her, cast himself at her feet, spoke the truth, and became, if he might, her slave for ever, failing which he could but turn and go wandering through the spheres, seeking rest and finding none, save indeed there were some salvation even for him in the bosom of his God—I say that, somehow, with all this on the brain and in the heart of him, the sunshine was yet pleasant to his eyes, while it stung him to the soul; the soft breathing of the wind was pleasant to his cheek, while he cursed himself for the pleasure it gave him; the few flowers that were left looked up at him mournfully and he let them look, nor turned his eyes away, but let the tears gather and flow. The first agonies of the encounter of life and death were over, and life was slowly wasting away. Oh what might not a little joy do for him! But where was the joy to be found that could irradiate such a darkness even for one fair memorial moment?

One hot noon Wingfold lay beside him on the grass. Neither had spoken for some time: the curate more and more shrunk from speech to which his heart was not directly moved. As to what might be in season or out of season, he never would pretend to judge, he said, but even Balaam's ass knew when he had a call to speak. He plucked a pale red pimpernel and handed it up over his head to Leopold. The youth looked at it for a moment, and burst into tears. The curate rose hastily.

"It is so heartless of me." said Leopold, "to take pleasure in such a childish innocence as this!"

"It merely shows," said the curate, laying his hand gently on his shoulder, "that even in these lowly lovelinesses, there is a something that has its root deeper than your pain; that, all about us, in earth and air, wherever eye or ear can reach, there is a power ever breathing itself forth in signs, now in a daisy, now in a windwaft, a cloud, a sunset; a power that holds constant and sweetest relation with the dark and silent world within us; that the same God who is in us, and upon whose tree we are the buds, if not yet the flowers, also is all about us—inside, the Spirit; outside, the Word. And the two are ever trying to meet in us; and when they meet, then the sign without, and the longing within, become one in light, and the man no more walketh in darkness, but knoweth whither he goeth."

As he ended thus, the curate bent over and looked at Leopold. But the poor boy had not listened to a word he said. Something in his tone had soothed him, but the moment he ceased, the vein of his grief burst out bleeding afresh. He clasped his thin hands together, and looked up in an agony of hopeless appeal to the blue sky, now grown paler as in fear of the coming cold, though still the air was warm and sweet, and cried,

"Oh! if God would only be good and unmake me, and let darkness cover the place where once was me! That would be like a good God! All I should be sorry for then would be, that there was not enough of me left for a dim flitting Will-o'-the-wisp of praise, ever singing my thankfulness to him that I was no more.—Yet even then my deed would remain, for I dare not ask that she should die outright also—that would be to heap wrong upon wrong. What an awful thing being is! Not even my annihilation could make up for my crime, or rid it out of the universe."

"True, Leopold!" said the curate. "Nothing but the burning love of God can rid sin out of anywhere. But are you not forgetting him who surely knew what he undertook when he would save the world? No more than you could have set that sun flaming overhead, with its million-miled billows and its limitless tempests of fire, can you tell what the love of God is, or what it can do for you, if only by enlarging your love with the inrush of itself. Few have such a cry to raise to the Father as you, such a claim of sin and helplessness to heave up before him, such a joy even to offer to the great Shepherd who cannot rest while one sheep strays from his flock, one prodigal haunts the dens of evil and waste. Cry to him, Leopold, my dear boy. Cry to him again and yet again, for he himself said that men ought always to pray and not faint, for God did hear and would answer although he might seem long about it. I think we shall find one day that nobody, not the poet of widest sweep and most daring imagination, not the prophet who soars the highest in his ardour to justify the ways of God to men, not the child when he is most fully possessed of the angel that in heaven always beholds the face of the Father of Jesus, has come or could have come within sight of the majesty of his bestowing upon his children. For did he not, if the story be true, allow torture itself to invade the very soul's citadel of his best beloved, as he went to seek the poor ape of a prodigal, stupidly grinning amongst his harlots?"

Leopold did not answer, and the shadow lay deep on his face for a while; but at length it began to thin, and at last a feeble quivering smile broke through the cloud, and he wept soft tears of refreshing.

It was not that the youth had turned again from the hope of rest in the Son of Man; but that, as everyone knows who knows anything of the human spirit, there must be in its history days and seasons, mornings and nights, yea deepest midnights. It has its alternating summer and winter, its storm and shine, its soft dews and its tempests of lashing hail, its cold moons and prophetic stars, its pale twilights of saddest memory, and its golden gleams of brightest hope. All these mingled and displaced each other in Leopold's ruined world, where chaos had come again, but over whose waters a mightier breath was now moving.

And now after much thought, the curate saw that he could not hope to transplant into the bosom of the lad the flowers of truth that gladdened his own garden: he must sow the seed from which they had sprung, and that seed was the knowledge of the true Jesus. It was now the more possible to help him in this way, that the wild beast of his despair had taken its claws from his bosom, had withdrawn a pace or two, and couched watching. And Wingfold soon found that nothing calmed and brightened him like talk about Jesus. He had tried verse first—seeking out the best within his reach wherein loving souls have uttered their devotion to the man of men; but here also the flowers would not be transplanted. How it came about he hardly knew, but he had soon drifted into rather than chosen another way, which way proved a right one: he would begin thinking aloud on some part of the gospel story, generally that which was most in his mind at the time—talking with himself, as it were, all about it. He began this one morning as he lay on the grass beside him, and that was the position in which he found he could best thus soliloquize. Now and then but not often Leopold would interrupt him, and perhaps turn the monologue into dialogue, but even then Wingfold would hardly ever look at him: he would not disturb him with more of his presence than he could help, or allow the truth to be flavoured with more of his individuality than was unavoidable. For every individuality, he argued, has a peculiar flavour to every other, and only Jesus is the pure simple humanity that every one can love, out and out, at once. In these mental meanderings, he avoided nothing, took notice of every difficulty, whether able to discuss it fully or not, broke out in words of delight when his spirit was moved, nor hid his disappointment when he failed in getting at what might seem good enough to be the heart of the thing. It was like hatching a sermon in the sun instead of in the oven. Occasionally, when, having ceased, he looked up to know how his pupil fared, he found him fast asleep—sometimes with a smile, sometimes with a tear on his face. The sight would satisfy him well. Calm upon such a tormented sea must be the gift of God; and the curate would then sometimes fall asleep himself—to start awake at the first far-off sound of Helen's dress as it swept a running fire of fairy fog-signals from the half-opened buds of the daisies, and the long heads of the rib-grass, when he would rise and saunter a few paces aside, and she would bend over her brother, to see if he were warm and comfortable. By this time all the old tenderness of her ministration had returned, nor did she seem any longer jealous of Wingfold's.

One day she came behind them as they talked. The grass had been mown that morning, and also she happened to be dressed in her riding- habit and had gathered up the skirt over her arm, so that on this occasion she made no sound of sweet approach. Wingfold had been uttering one of his rambling monologues—in which was much without form, but nothing void.

"I don't know quite," he had been saying, "what to think about that story of the woman they brought to Jesus in the temple—I mean how it got into that nook of the gospel of St. John, where it has no right place.—They didn't bring her for healing or for the rebuke of her demon, but for condemnation, only they came to the wrong man for that. They dared not carry out the law of stoning, as they would have liked, I suppose, even if Jesus had condemned her, but perhaps they hoped rather to entrap him who was the friend of sinners into saying something against the law.—But what I want is, to know how it got there,—just there, I mean, betwixt the seventh and eighth chapters of St. John's Gospel. There is no doubt of its being an interpolation—that the twelfth verse, I think it is, ought to join on to the fifty-second. The Alexandrian manuscript is the only one of the three oldest that has it, and it is the latest of the three. I did think once, but hastily, that it was our Lord's text for saying I AM THE LIGHT OF THE WORLD, but it follows quite as well on his offer of living water. One can easily see how the place would appear a very suitable one to any presumptuous scribe who wished to settle the question of where it should stand.—I wonder if St. John told the lovely tale as something he had forgotten, after he had finished dictating all the rest. Or was it well known to all the evangelists, only no one of them was yet partaker enough of the spirit of him who was the friend of sinners, to dare put it on written record, thinking it hardly a safe story to expose to the quarrying of men's conclusions? But it doesn't matter much: the tale must be a true one. Only—to think of just this one story, of tenderest righteousness, floating about like a holy waif through the world of letters!—a sweet gray dove of promise that can find no rest for the sole of his foot! Just this one story of all stories a kind of outcast! and yet as a wanderer, oh, how welcome! Some manuscripts, I understand, have granted it a sort of outhouse-shelter at the end of the gospel of St. Luke. But it all matters nothing, so long as we can believe it; and true it must be, it is so like him all through. And if it does go wandering as a stray through the gospels, without place of its own, what matters it so long as it can find hearts enough to nestle in, and bring forth its young of comfort!—Perhaps the woman herself told it, and, as with the woman of Samaria, some would and some would not believe her.—Oh! the eyes that met upon her! The fiery hail of scorn from those of the Pharisees—

the light of eternal sunshine from those of Jesus!—I was reading the other day, in one of the old Miracle Plays, how each that looked on while Jesus wrote with his finger on the ground, imagined he was writing down his individual sins, and was in terror lest his neighbour should come to know them.—And wasn't he gentle even with those to whom he was sharper than a two-edged sword! and oh how gentle to her he would cover from their rudeness and wrong! LET THE SINLESS THROW! And the sinners went out, and she followed—to sin no more. No reproaches, you see! No stirring up of the fiery snakes! Only don't do it again.—I don't think she did it again:—do you?"

It was just here that Helen came and stood behind Leopold's chair. The curate lay on the grass, and neither saw her.

CHAPTER XVI.

HOW JESUS SPOKE TO WOMEN.

"But why wasn't he as gentle with good women?" said Leopold.

"Wasn't he?" said the curate in some surprise.

"He said What have I to do with thee to his own mother?"

"A Greek scholar should go to the Greek," said the curate. "Our English is not perfect. You see she wanted to make him show off, and he thought how little she knew what he came to the world for. Her thoughts were so unlike his that he said, What have we in common! It was a moan of the God-head over the distance of its creature. Perhaps he thought: How then will you stand the shock when at length it comes? But he looked at her as her own son ought to look at every blessed mother, and she read in his eyes no rebuke, for instantly, sure of her desire, she told them to do whatever he said."

"I hope that's the right way of it," said Leopold, "for I want to trust him out and out. But what do you make of the story of the poor woman that came about her daughter? Wasn't he rough to her? It always seemed to me such a cruel thing to talk of throwing the meat of the children to the dogs!"

"We cannot judge of the word until we know the spirit that gave birth to it. Let me ask you a question: What would you take for the greatest proof of downright friendship a man could show you?"

"That is too hard a question to answer all at once."

"Well, I may be wrong, but the deepest outcome of friendship seems to me, on the part of the superior at least, the permission, or better still, the call, to share in his sufferings. And in saying that hard word to the poor Gentile, our Lord honoured her thus mightily. He assumed for the moment the part of the Jew towards the Gentile, that he might, for the sake of all the world of Gentiles and Jews, lay bare to his Jewish followers the manner of spirit they were of, and let them see what a lovely humanity they despised in their pride of election. He took her to suffer with him for the salvation of the world. The cloud overshadowed them both, but what words immediately thereafter made a glory in her heart! He spoke to her as if her very faith had reached an arm into the heavens, and brought therefrom the thing she sought.—But I confess," the curate went on, "those two passages have both troubled me. So I presume will everything that is God's, until it becomes a strength and a light by revealing its true nature to the heart that has grown capable of understanding it. The first sign of the coming capacity and the coming joy, is the anxiety and the question.—There is another passage, which, although it does not trouble me so much, I cannot yet get a right perception of. When Mary Magdalene took the Master of Death for the gardener—the gardener of the garden of the tombs! no great mistake, was it?—it is a lovely thing, that mistaking of Jesus for the gardener!—how the holy and the lowly, yea the holy and the common meet on all sides! Just listen to their morning talk— the morning of the eternal open world to Jesus, while the shadows of this narrow life still clustered around Mary:—I can give it you exactly, for I was reading it this very day.

"'Woman, why weepest thou? Whom seekest thou?'

"'Sir, if thou have borne him hence, tell me where thou hast laid him, and I will take him away.'

"'Mary.'

"'Master!'

"'Touch me not; for I am not yet ascended to my Father: but go to my brethren, and say unto them, I ascend unto my Father and your Father; and to my God and your God.'

"Why did he say, DO NOT TOUCH ME? It could not be that there was any defilement to one in the new body of the resurrection, from contact with one still in the old garments of humanity. But could it be that there was danger to her in the contact? Was there something in the new house from Heaven hurtful to the old tabernacle? I can hardly believe it. Perhaps it might be. But we must look at the reason the Master gives—only of all words hard to understand, the little conjunctions are sometimes the hardest. What can that FOR mean? 'Touch me not, FOR I am not yet ascended to my Father.' Does it mean, 'I must first present myself to my Father; I must first have His hand laid on this body new-risen from the grave; I must go home first?' The child must kiss his mother first, then his sisters and brothers: was it so with Jesus? Was he so glad in his father, that he must carry even the human body he had rescued eternal from the grave, home to show him first? There are many difficulties about the interpretation, and even if true, it would still shock every heart whose devotion was less than absolutely child-like. Was not God WITH him, as close to him as even God could come to his eternal son—in him—ONE with him, all the time? How could he get nearer to him by going to Heaven? What head-quarters, what court of place and circumstance should the Eternal, Immortal, Invisible hold? And yet if from him flow time and space, although he cannot be subject to them; if his son could incarnate himself—cast the living, responsive, elastic, flowing, evanishing circumstance of a human garment around him; if, as Novalis says, God can become whatever he can create, then may there not be some central home of God, holding relation even to time and space and sense? But I am bewildered about it.—Jesus stood then in the meeting point of both worlds, or rather in the skirts of the great world that infolds the less. I am talking like a baby, for my words cannot compass or even represent my thoughts. This world looks to us the natural and simple one, and so it is—absolutely fitted to our need and education. But there is that in us which is not at home in this world, which I believe holds secret relations with every star, or perhaps rather, with that in the heart of God whence issued every star, diverse in kind and character as in colour and place and motion and light. To that in us, this world is so far strange and unnatural and unfitting, and we need a yet homelier home. Yea, no home at last will do, but the home of God's heart. Jesus, I say, was now looking, on one side, into the region of a deeper life, where his people, those that knew their own when they saw him, would one day find themselves tenfold at home; while, on the other hand, he was looking into the region of their present life, which custom and faithlessness make them afraid to leave. But we need not fear what the new conditions of life will bring, either for body or heart, for they will be nearer and sweeter to our deeper being, as Jesus is nearer and dearer than any man because he is more human than any. He is all that we can love or look for, and at the root of that very loving and looking.—'In my Father's house are many mansions,' he said. Matter, time, space, are all God's, and whatever may become of our philosophies, whatever he does with or in respect of time, place, and what we call matter, his doing must be true in philosophy as well as fact. But I am wandering."

The curate was wandering, but the liberty of wandering was essential to his talking with the kind of freedom and truth he wanted to mediate betwixt his pupil and the lovely things he saw.

"I wonder where the penitent thief was all the time," said Leopold.

"Yes, that also is a difficulty. There again come in the bothering time and space, bothering in their relation to heavenly things, I mean. On the Friday, the penitent thief, as you call him, was to be with Jesus in Paradise; and now it was Sunday, and Jesus said he had not yet been up to see his Father. Some would say, I am too literal, too curious; what can Friday and Sunday have to do with Paradise? But words MEAN in both worlds, for they are not two but one—surely at least when Jesus thinks and speaks of them; and there can be no wrong in feeling ever so blindly and dully after WHAT they mean. Such humble questioning can do no harm, even if, in face of the facts, the questions be as far off and SILLY—in the old sweet meaning of the word— as those of any infant concerning a world he has not proved.—But about Mary Magdalene: He must have said the word TOUCH ME NOT. That could not have crept in. It is too hard for an interpolation, I think; and if no interpolation, it must mean some deep-good thing we don't understand. One thing we can make sure of: it was nothing that should hurt her; for see what follows. But for that, when he said TOUCH ME NOT, FOR I AM NOT YET ASCENDED TO MY FATHER, she might have thought—'Ah! thou hast thy Father to go to, and thou wilt leave us for him.'—BUT, he went on,

GO TO MY BRETHREN AND SAY UNTO THEM: I ASCEND UNTO MY FATHER, AND YOUR FATHER; AND MY GOD AND YOUR GOD. What more could she want? Think: the Father of Jesus, with whom, in all his knowledge and all his suffering, the grand heart was perfectly, exultingly satisfied,—that Father he calls our Father too. He shares with his brethren—of his best, his deepest, his heartiest, most secret delight, and makes it their and his most open joy: he shares his eternal Father with us, his perfect God with his brethren. And whatever his not having yet ascended to him may mean, we see, with marvel and joy, that what delayed him—even though, for some reason perfect in tenderness as in truth, he would not be touched—was love to Mary Magdalene and his mother and his brethren. He could not go to the Father without comforting them first. And certainly whatever she took the TOUCH ME NOT to mean or point at, it was nothing that hurt her.—It just strikes me—is it possible he said it in order to turn the overwhelming passion of her joy, which after such a restoration would have clung more than ever to the visible presence, and would be ready to suffer the pains of death yet again when he parted from her—might it be to turn that torrent into the wider and ever widening channel of joy in his everlasting presence to the innermost being, his communion, heart to heart, with every child of his Father? In our poor weakness and narrowness and self-love, even of Jesus the bodily may block out the spiritual nearness, which, however in most moods we may be unable to realise the fact, is and remains a thing unutterably lovelier and better and dearer—enhancing tenfold what vision of a bodily presence may at some time be granted us. But how any woman can help casting herself heart and soul at the feet of such a lowly grandeur, such a tender majesty, such a self-dissolving perfection—I cannot imagine. The truth must be that those who kneel not have not seen. You do not once read of a woman being against him—except indeed it was his own mother, when she thought he was going all astray and forgetting his high mission. The divine love in him towards his Father in heaven and his brethren of men, was ever melting down his conscious individuality in sweetest showers upon individual hearts; he came down like rain upon the mown grass, like showers that water the earth. No woman, no man surely ever saw him as he was and did not worship!"

Helen turned and glided back into the house, and neither knew she had been there.

CHAPTER XVII.

DELIVERANCE.

All that could be done for Leopold by tenderest sisterly care under the supervision of Mr. Faber, who believed in medicine less than in good nursing, was well supplemented by the brotherly ministrations of Wingfold, who gave all the time he could honestly spare from his ordinary work to soothe and enlighten the suffering youth. But it became clearer every week that nothing would avail to entice the torn roots of his being to clasp again the soil of the world: he was withering away out of it. Ere long symptoms appeared which no one could well mistake, and Lingard himself knew that he was dying. Wingfold had dreaded that his discovery of the fact might reveal that he had imagined some atonement in the public confession he desired to make, and that, when he found it denied him, he would fall into despair. But he was with him at the moment, and his bearing left no ground for anxiety. A gleam of gladness from below the horizon of his spirit, shot up, like the aurora of a heavenly morning, over the sky of his countenance. He glanced at his friend, smiled, and said,

"It has killed me too, and that is a comfort."

The curate only looked his reply.

"They say," resumed Leopold, after a while, "that God takes the will for the deed:—do you think so?"

"Certainly, if it be a true, genuine will."

"I am sure I meant to give myself up," said Leopold. "I had not the slightest idea they were fooling me. I know it now, but what can I do? I am so weak, I should only die on the way."

He tried to rise, but fell back in the chair.

"Oh!" he sighed, "isn't it good of God to let me die! Who knows what he may do for me on the other side! Who can tell what the bounty of a God like Jesus may be!"

A vision arose before the mind's eye of the curate:—Emmeline kneeling for Leopold's forgiveness; but he wisely held his peace. The comforter of the sinner must come from the forgiveness of God, not from the favourable judgment of man mitigating the harshness of his judgment of himself. Wingfold's business was to start him well in the world whither he was going. He must fill his scrip with the only wealth that would not dissolve in the waters of the river—that was, the knowledge of Jesus.

It shot a terrible pang to the heart of Helen, herself, for all her suffering, so full of life, when she learned that her darling must die. Yet was there no small consolation mingled with the shock. Fear vanished, and love returned with grief in twofold strength. She flew to him, and she who had been so self-contained, so composed, so unsubmissive to any sway of feeling, broke into such a storm of passionate affection that the vexilla mortis answered from his bosom, flaunting themselves in crimson before her eyes. In vain, for Leopold's sake, the curate had sought to quiet her: she had resented his interference; but this result of her impetuosity speedily brought her to her senses, and set her to subdue herself.

The same evening Leopold insisted on dictating to the curate his confession, which done, he signed it, making him and Helen attest the signature. This document Wingfold took charge of, promising to make the right use of it, whatever he should on reflection conclude that to be; after which Leopold's mind seemed at ease.

His sufferings from cough and weakness and fever now augmented with greater rapidity, but it was plain from the kind of light in his eye, and the far look which was not yet retrospective, that hope and expectation were high in him. He had his times of gloom, when the dragon of the past crept out of its cave, and tore him afresh; but the prospect of coming deliverance strengthened him.

"Do you really think," he said once to the curate, "that I shall ever see Emmeline again?"

"Truly I hope so," answered his friend, "and could argue upon the point. But I think the best way, when doubt comes as to anything you would like to be true, is just to hide yourself in God, as the child would hide from the dark in the folds of his mother's mantle."

"But aunt would say, if she knew, that, dying as she did, Emmeline could not be saved."

"Some people may have to be a good deal astonished as to what can and cannot be," returned the curate. "But never mind what people say: make your appeal to the saviour of men about whatever troubles you. Cry to the faithful creator, his Father. To be a faithful creator needs a might of truth and loving-kindness of which our narrow hearts can ill conceive. Ask much of God, my boy, and be very humble and very hoping."

After all such utterances, Leopold would look his thanks, and hold his peace.

"I wish it was over," he said once.

"So do I," returned the curate. "But be of good courage, I think nothing will be given you to bear that you will not be able to bear."

"I can bear a great deal more than I have had yet. I don't think I shall ever complain. That would be to take myself out of his hands, and I have no hope anywhere else.—Are you any surer about him, sir, than you used to be?"

"At least I hope in him far more," answered Wingfold.

"Is that enough?"

"No. I want more."

"I wish I could come back and tell you that I am alive and all is true."

"I would rather have the natural way of it, and get the good of not knowing first."

"But if I could tell you I had found God, then that would make you sure."

Wingfold could not help a smile:—as if any assurance from such a simple soul could reach the questions that tossed his troubled spirit!

"I think I shall find all I want in Jesus Christ," he said.

"But you can't see him, you know."

"Perhaps I can do better. And at all events I can wait," said the curate. "Even if he would let me, I would not see him one moment before he thought it best. I would not be out of a doubt or difficulty an hour sooner than he would take me."

Leopold gazed at him and said no more.

CHAPTER XVIII.

THE MEADOW.

As the disease advanced, his desire for fresh air and freedom grew to a great longing. One hot day, whose ardours, too strong for the leaves whose springs had begun to dry up, were burning them "yellow and black and pale and hectic red," the fancy seized him to get out of the garden with its clipt box-trees and cypresses, into the meadow beyond. There a red cow was switching her tail as she gathered her milk from the world, and looking as if all were well. He liked the look of the cow, and the open meadow, and wanted to share it with her, he said. Helen, with the anxiety of a careful nurse, feared it might hurt him.

"What DOES it matter?" he returned. "Is life so sweet that every moment more of it is a precious boon? After I'm gone a few days, you won't know a week from an hour of me. What a weight it will be off you! I envy you all the relief of it. It will be to you just what it would be to me to get into that meadow."

Helen made haste to let him have his will. They prepared a sort of litter, and the curate and the coachman carried him. Hearing what they were about, Mrs. Ramshorn hurried into the garden to protest, but protested in vain, and joined the little procession, walking with Helen, like a second mourner, after the bier. They crossed the lawn, and through a double row of small cypresses went winding down to the underground passage, as if to the tomb itself. They had not thought of opening the door first, and the place was dark and sepulchral. Helen hastened to set it wide.

"Lay me down for a moment," said Leopold. "—Here I lie in my tomb! How soft and brown the light is! I should not mind lying here, half-asleep, half-awake, for centuries, if only I had the hope of a right good waking at last."

A flood of fair light flashed in sweet torrent into the place—and there, framed in the doorway, but far across the green field, stood the red cow, switching her tail.

"And here comes my resurrection!" cried Leopold. "I have not had long to wait for it—have I?"

He smiled a pained content as he spoke, and they bore him out into the sun and air. They set him down in the middle of the field in a low chair—not far from a small clump of trees, through which the footpath led to the stile whereon the curate was seated when he first saw the Polwarths. Mrs. Ramshorn found the fancy of the sick man pleasant for the hale, and sent for her knitting. Helen sat down empty-handed on the wool at her brother's feet, and Wingfold, taking a book from his pocket, withdrew to the trees.

He had not read long, sitting within sight and call of the group, when Helen came to him.

"He seems inclined to go to sleep," she said. "Perhaps if you would read something, it would send him off."

"I will with pleasure," he said, and returning with her, sat down on the grass.

"May I read you a few verses I came upon the other day, Leopold?" he asked.

"Please do," answered the invalid, rather sleepily.

I will not pledge myself that the verses belonged to the book Wingfold held before him, but here they are. He read them slowly, and as evenly and softly and rhythmically as he could.

> They come to thee, the halt, the maimed, the blind,
>   The devil-torn, the sick, the sore;
> Thy heart their well of life they find,
>   Thine ear their open door.
>
> Ah! who can tell the joy in Palestine—
>   What smiles and tears of rescued throngs!
> Their lees of life were turned to wine,
>   Their prayers to shouts and songs!
>
> The story dear our wise men fable call,
>   Give paltry facts the mighty range;
> To me it seems just what should fall,
>   And nothing very strange.
>
> But were I deaf and lame and blind and sore,
>   I scarce would care for cure to ask;
> Another prayer should haunt thy door—
>   Set thee a harder task.
>
> If thou art Christ, see here this heart of mine,
>   Torn, empty, moaning, and unblest!
> Had ever heart more need of thine,
>   If thine indeed hath rest?
>
> Thy word, thy hand right soon did scare the bane
>   That in their bodies death did breed:
> If thou canst cure my deeper pain,
>   Then thou art Lord indeed.

Leopold smiled sleepily as Wingfold read, and ere the reading was over, slept.

"What can the little object want here?" said Mrs. Ramshorn.

Wingfold looked up, and seeing who it was approaching them, said,

"Oh! that is Mr. Polwarth, who keeps the park gate."

"Nobody can well mistake him," returned Mrs. Ramshorn. "Everybody knows the creature."

"Few people know him really," said Wingfold.

"I HAVE heard that he is an oddity in mind as well as in body," said Mrs. Ramshorn.

"He is a friend of mine," rejoined the curate. "I will go and meet him. He wants to know how Leopold is."

"Pray keep your seat, Mr. Wingfold. I don't in the least mind him," said Mrs. Ramshorn. "Any FRIEND of yours, as you are kind enough to call him, will be welcome. Clergymen come to know—indeed it is their duty to be acquainted with all sorts of people. The late dean of Halystone would stop and speak to a pauper."

The curate did however go and meet Polwarth, and returning with him presented him to Mrs. Ramshorn, who received him with perfect condescension, and a most gracious bow. Helen bent her head also, very differently, but it would be hard to say how. The little man turned from them, and for a moment stood looking on the face of the sleeping youth: he had not seen him since Helen ordered him to leave the house. Even now she looked angry at his presumption in staring at her brother. But Polwarth did not see her look. A great tenderness came over his face, and his lips moved softly. "The Lord of thy life keep it for thee, my son!" he murmured, gazed a moment longer, then rejoined Wingfold.

They walked aside a few paces.

"Pray be seated," said Mrs. Ramshorn, without looking up from her knitting—the seat she offered being the wide meadow.

But they had already done so, and presently were deep in a gentle talk, of which at length certain words that had been foolhardy enough to wander within her range, attracted the notice of Mrs. Ramshorn, and she began to listen. But she could not hear distinctly.

"There should be one bishop at least," the little man was saying, "or I don't know but he ought to be the arch-arch-bishop,—a poor man, if possible,— one like the country parson Chaucer sets up in contrast with the regular clergy,—whose main business should be to travel about from university to university, from college to college, from school to school, warning off all young men who did not know within themselves that it was neither for position, nor income, nor study, nor influence, that they sought to minister in the temple, from entering the church. As from holy ground, he would warn them off."

Mrs. Ramshorn fancied, from certain obscure associations in her own mind, that he was speaking of dissenting ministers and persons of low origin, who might wish to enter the church for the sake of BETTERING THEMSELVES, and holding as she did, that no church preferment should be obtained except by persons of good family and position, qualified to keep up the dignity of the profession, she was not a little gratified to hear, as she supposed, the same sentiments from the mouth of such an illiterate person as, taking no note of his somewhat remarkable utterance, she imagined Polwarth to be. Therefore she proceeded to patronize him yet a little farther.

"I quite agree with you," she said graciously. "None but such as you describe should presume to set foot within the sacred precincts of the profession."

Polwarth did not much relish Mrs. Ramshorn's style, and was considerably surprised at receiving such a hearty approval of a proposed reformation in clerical things, reaching even to the archiepiscopal, which he had put half-humorously, and yet in thorough earnest, for the ear of Wingfold only. He was little enough desirous of pursuing the conversation with Mrs. Ramshorn: Charity herself does not require of a man to cast his precious things at the feet of my lady Disdain; but he must reply.

"Yes," he said, "the great evil in the church has always been the presence in it of persons unsuited for the work there required of them. One very simple sifting rule would be, that no one should be admitted to holy orders who had not first proved himself capable of making a better living in some other calling."

"I cannot go with you so far as that—so few careers are opened to gentlemen," rejoined Mrs. Ramshorn. "Besides—take the bar, for instance: the forensic style a man must there acquire would hardly become the pulpit. But it would not be a bad rule that everyone, for admission to holy orders, should be possessed of property sufficient at least to live upon. With that for a foundation, his living would begin at once to tell, and he would immediately occupy the superior position every clergyman ought to have."

"What I was thinking of," said Polwarth, "was mainly the experience in life he would gather by having to make his own living; that, behind the counter or the plough, or in the workshop, he would come to know men and their struggles and their thoughts—"

"Good heavens!" exclaimed Mrs. Ramshorn. "But I must be under some misapprehension! It is not possible you can be speaking of the CHURCH— of the clerical PROFESSION. The moment that is brought within the reach of such people as you describe, that moment the church sinks to the level of the catholic priesthood."

"Say rather, to the level of Jeremy Taylor," returned Polwarth, "who was the son of a barber; or of Tillotson, who was the son of a clothier, or something of the sort, and certainly a fierce dissenter. His enemies said the archbishop himself was never baptized. By-the-way, he was not ordained till he was thirty—and that bears on what I was just saying to Mr. Wingfold, that I would have no one ordained till after forty, by which time he would know whether he had any real call or only a temptation to the church, from the base hope of an easy living."

By this time Mrs. Ramshorn had had more than enough of it. The man was a leveller, a chartist, a positivist—a despiser of dignities!

"Mr.—, Mr.—, I don't know your name—you will oblige me by uttering no more such vile slanders in my company. You are talking about what you don't in the least understand. The man who does not respect the religion of his native country is capable of—of—of ANYTHING.—I am astonished, Mr. Wingfold, at your allowing a member of your congregation to speak with so little regard for the feelings of the clergy.—You forget, sir, when you attribute what you call base motives to the cloth—you forget who said the labourer was worthy of his hire."

"I hope not, madam. I only venture to suggest that, though the labourer is worthy of his hire, not every man is worthy of the labour."

Wingfold was highly amused at the turn things had taken. Polwarth looked annoyed at having allowed himself to be beguiled into such an utterly useless beating of the air.

"My friend HAS some rather peculiar notions, Mrs. Ramshorn," said the curate;" but you must admit it was your approval that encouraged him to go on."

"It is quite as well to know what people think," answered Mrs. Ramshorn, pretending she had drawn him out from suspicion. "My husband used to say that very few of the clergy had any notion of the envy and opposition of the lower orders, both to them personally, and to the doctrines they taught. To low human nature the truth has always been unpalatable."

What precisely she meant by THE TRUTH it would be hard to say, but if the visual embodiment of it was not a departed dean, it was at least always associated in her mind with a cathedral choir, and a portly person in silk stockings.

Here happily Leopold woke, and his eyes fell upon the gate-keeper.

"Ah, Mr. Polwarth! I am so glad to see you!" he said." I am getting on, you see. It will be over soon."

"I see," replied Polwarth, going up to him, and taking his offered hand in both his. "I could almost envy you for having got so near the end of your troubles."

"Are you sure it will be the end of them, sir?"

"Of some of them at least, I hope, and those the worst. I cannot be sure of anything but that all things work together for good to them that love God."

"I don't know yet whether I do love God."

"Not the father of Jesus Christ?"

"If God is really just like him, I don't see how any man could help loving him. But, do you know? I am terrified sometimes at the thought of seeing MY father. He was such a severe man! I am afraid he will scorn me."

"Never—if he has got into heavenly ways. And you have your mother there too, have you not?"

"Oh! yes; I didn't think of that. I don't remember much of her."

"Anyhow, you have God there, and you must rest in him. He will not forget you, for that would be ceasing to be God. If God were to forget for one moment, the universe would grow black—vanish—rush out again from the realm of law and order into chaos and night."

"But I have been wicked."

"The more need you have, if possible, of your Father in heaven."

Here Mrs. Ramshorn beckoned the attendance of the curate where she sat a few yards off on the other side of Leopold. She was a little ashamed of having condescended to lose her temper, and when the curate went up to her, said, with an attempt at gaiety:

"Is your odd little friend, as you call him, all—?"

And she tapped her lace-cap carefully with her finger.

"Rather more so than most people," answered Wingfold. "He is a very remarkable man."

"He speaks as if he had seen better days—though where he can have gathered such detestable revolutionary notions, I can't think."

"He is a man of education, as you see," said the curate.

"You don't mean he has been to Oxford or Cambridge?"

"No. His education has been of a much higher sort than is generally found there. He knows ten times as much as most university men."

"Ah! yes; but that goes for nothing: he hasn't the standing. And if he had been to Oxford, he never could have imbibed such notions. Besides—his manners! To speak of the clergy as he did in the hearing of one whose whole history is bound up with the church!"

She meant herself, not Wingfold.

"But of course," she went on, "there must be something VERY wrong with him to know so much as you say, and occupy such a menial position! Nothing but a gate-keeper, and talk like that about bishops and what not! People that are crooked in body are always crooked in mind too. I dare say now he has quite a coterie of friends and followers amongst the lower orders in Glaston. He's just the sort of man to lead the working classes astray. No doubt he is a very interesting study for a young man like you, but you must take care; you may be misunderstood. A young clergyman CAN'T be too cautious—if he has any hope of rising in his profession.—A gate-keeper, indeed!"

"Wasn't it something like that David wanted to be?" said the curate.

"Mr. Wingfold, I never allow any such foolish jests in my hearing. It was a DOOR-keeper the Psalmist said—and to the house of God, not a nobleman's park."

"A verger, I suppose," thought Wingfold.—"Seriously, Mrs. Ramshorn, that poor little atom of a creature is the wisest man I know," he said.

"Likely enough, in YOUR judgment, Mr. Wingfold," said the dean's widow, and drew herself up.

The curate accepted his dismissal, and joined the little man by Leopold's chair.

"I wish you two could be with me when I am dying," said Leopold.

"If you will let your sister know your wish, you may easily have it," said the curate.

"It will be just like saying good-bye at the pier-head, and pushing off alone— you can't get more than one into the boat—out, out, alone, into the infinite ocean of—nobody knows what or where," said Leopold.

"Except those that are there already, and they will be waiting to receive you," said Polwarth. "You may well hope, if you have friends to see you off, you will have friends to welcome you too. But I think it's not so much like setting off from the pier-head, as getting down the side of the ocean-ship, to laud at the pier-head, where your friends are all standing looking out for you."

"Well! I don't know," said Leopold, with a sigh of weariness. "I'm thankful sometimes that I've grown stupid. I suppose it's with dying. I didn't use to feel so. Sometimes I seem not to know or care anything about anything. I only want to stop coughing and aching and go to sleep."

"Jesus was glad to give up his spirit into his Father's hands. He was very tired before he got away."

"Thank you. Thank you. I have him. He is somewhere. You can't mention his name but it brings me something to live and hope for. If he is there, all will be well. And if I do get too tired to care for anything, he won't mind; he will only let me go to sleep, and wake me up again by-and-by when I am rested."

He closed his eyes.

"I want to go to bed," he said.

They carried him into the house.

CHAPTER XIX.

RACHEL AND LEOPOLD.

Every day after this, so long as the weather continued warm, it was Leopold's desire to be carried out to the meadow. Once at his earnest petition, instead of setting him down in the usual place, they went on with him into the park, but he soon wished to be taken back to the meadow. He did not like the trees to come between him and his bed: they made him feel like a rabbit that was too far from its hole, he said; and he was never tempted to try it again.

Regularly too every day, about one o'clock, the gnome-like form of the gate-keeper would issue from the little door in the park-fence, and come marching across the grass towards Leopold's chair, which was set near the small clump of trees already mentioned. The curate was almost always there, not talking much to the invalid, but letting him know every now and then by some little attention or word, or merely by showing himself, that he was near. Sometimes he would take refuge from the heat, which the Indian never felt too great, amongst the trees, and there would generally be thinking out what he wanted to say to his people the next Sunday.

One thing he found strange, and could not satisfy himself concerning, namely, that although his mind was so much occupied with Helen that he often seemed unable to think consecutively upon any subject, he could always foresee his sermon best when, seated behind one of the trees, he could by moving his head see her at work beside Leopold's chair. But the thing that did carry him through became plain enough to him afterwards: his faith in God was all the time growing—and that through what seemed at the time only a succession of interruptions. Nothing is so ruinous to progress in which effort is needful, as satisfaction with apparent achievement; that ever sounds a halt; but Wingfold's experience was that no sooner did he set his foot on the lowest hillock of self-congratulation than some fresh difficulty came that threw him prostrate; and he rose again only in the strength of the necessity for deepening and broadening his foundations that he might build yet higher, trust yet farther: that was the only way not to lose everything. He was gradually learning that his faith must be an absolute one, claiming from God everything the love of a perfect Father could give, or the needs he had created in his child could desire; that he must not look to himself first for help, or imagine that the divine was only the supplement to the weakness and failure of the human; that the highest effort of the human was to lay hold of the divine. He learned that he could keep no simplest law in its loveliness until he was possessed of the same spirit whence that law sprung; that he could not love Helen aright, simply, perfectly, unselfishly, except through the presence of the originating Love; that the one thing wherein he might imitate the free creative will of God was to will the presence and power of that will which gave birth to his. It was the vital growth of this faith, even when he was too much troubled to recognize the fact, that made him strong in the midst of weakness; when the son of man in him cried out, Let this cup pass, the son of God in him could yet cry, Let thy will be done. He could "inhabit trembling," and yet be brave.

Mrs. Ramshorn generally came to the meadow to see how the invalid was after he was settled, but she seldom staid: she was not fond of nursing, neither was there any need of her assistance; and as Helen never dreamed now of opposing the smallest wish of her brother, there was no longer any obstruction to the visits of Polwarth, which were eagerly looked for by Leopold.

One day the little man did not appear, but soon after his usual time the still more gnome-like form of his little niece came scrambling rather than walking over the meadow. Gently and modestly, almost shyly, she came up to Helen, made her a courtesy like a village school-girl, and said, while she glanced at Leopold now and then with an ocean of tenderness in her large, clear woman-eyes:

"My uncle is sorry, Miss Lingard, that he cannot come to see your brother to-day, but he is laid up with an attack of asthma. He wished Mr. Lingard to know that he was thinking of him:—shall I tell you just what he said?"

Helen bent her neck: she did not feel much interest in the matter. But Leopold said,

"Every word of such a good man is precious: tell me, please."

Rachel turned to him with the flush of a white rose on her face.

"I asked him, sir—'Shall I tell him you are praying for him?' and he said, 'No. I am not exactly praying for him, but I am thinking of God and him together.'"

The tears rose in Leopold's eyes. Rachel lifted her baby-hand, and stroked the dusky, long-fingured one that lay upon the arm of the chair.

"Dear Mr. Lingard," she said,—Helen stopped in the middle of an embroidery stitch, and gave her a look as if she were about to ask for her testimonials—"I could well wish, if it pleased God, that I were as near home as you."

Leopold took her hand in his.

"Do you suffer then?" he said.

"Just look at me," she answered with a smile that was very pitiful, though she did not mean it for such, "—shut up all my life in this epitome of deformity!

But I ain't grumbling: that would be a fine thing! My house is not so small but God can get into it. Only you can't think how tired I often am of it."

"Mr. Wingfold was telling me yesterday that some people fancy St. Paul was little and misshapen, and that that was his thorn in the flesh."

"I don't think that can be true, or he would never have compared his body to a tabernacle, for, oh dear! it won't stretch an inch to give a body room. I don't think either, if that had been the case, he would have said he didn't want it taken off, but another put over it. I do want mine taken off me, and a downright good new one put on instead—something not quite so far off your sister's there, Mr. Lingard. But I'm ashamed of talking like this. It came of wanting to tell you I can't be sorry you are going when I should so dearly like to go myself."

"And I would gladly stay a while, and that in a house no bigger than yours, if I had a conscience of the same sort in my back-parlour," said Leopold smiling. "But when I am gone the world will be the cleaner for it.—Do you know about God the same way your uncle does, Miss Polwarth?"

"I hope I do—a little. I doubt if anybody knows as much as he does," she returned, very seriously. "But God knows about us all the same, and he don't limit his goodness to us by our knowledge of him. It's so wonderful that he can be all to everybody! That is his Godness, you know. We can't be all to any one person. Do what we will, we can't let anybody see into us even. We are all in bits and spots. But I fancy it's a sign that we come of God that we don't like it. How gladly I would help you, Mr. Lingard, and I can do nothing for you.—I'm afraid your beautiful sister thinks me very forward. But she don't know what it is to lie awake all night sometimes, think-thinking about my beautiful brothers and sisters that I can't get near to do anything for."

"What an odd creature!" thought Helen, to whom her talk conveyed next to nothing. "—But I daresay they are both out of their minds. Poor things! they must have a hard time of it with one thing and another!"

"I beg your pardon again for talking so much," concluded Rachel, and, with a courtesy first to the one then to the other, walked away. Her gait was no square march like her uncle's, but a sort of sidelong propulsion, rendered more laborious by the thick grass of the meadow.

CHAPTER XX.

THE BLOOD-HOUND.

I need not follow the steps by which the inquiry-office became able so far to enlighten the mother of Emmeline concerning the person and habits of the visitor to the deserted shaft, that she had now come to Glaston in pursuit of yet farther discovery concerning him. She had no plan in her mind, and as yet merely intended going to church and everywhere else where people congregated, in the hope of something turning up to direct inquiry. Not a suspicion of Leopold had ever crossed her. She did not even know that he had a sister in Glaston, for Emmeline's friends had not all been intimate with her parents.

On the morning after her arrival, she went out early to take a walk, and brood over her cherished vengeance; and finding her way into the park, wandered about in it for some time. Leaving it at length by another gate, and inquiring the way to Glaston, she was directed to a footpath which would lead her thither across the fields. Following this, she came to a stile, and being rather weary with her long walk, sat down on it.

The day was a grand autumnal one. But nature had no charms for her. Indeed had she not been close shut in the gloomy chamber of her own thoughts, she would not thus have walked abroad alone; for nature was to her a dull, featureless void; while her past was scarcely of the sort to invite retrospection, and her future was clouded.

It so fell that just then Leopold was asleep in his chair,—every morning he slept a little soon after being carried out,—and that chair was in its usual place in the meadow, with the clump of trees between it and the stile. Wingfold was seated in the shade of the trees, but Helen, happening to want something for her work, went to him and committed her brother to his care until she should return, whereupon he took her place. Almost the same moment however, he spied Polwarth coming from the little door in the fence, and went to meet him. When he turned, he saw, to his surprise, a lady standing beside the sleeping youth, and gazing at him with a strange intentness. Polwarth had seen her come from the clump of trees, and supposed her a friend. The curate walked hastily back, fearing he might wake and be startled at sight of the stranger. So intent was the gazing lady that he was within a few yards of her before she heard him. She started, gave one glance at the curate, and hurried away towards the town. There was an agitation in her movements which Wingfold did not like; a suspicion crossed his mind, and he resolved to follow her. In his turn he made over his charge to Polwarth, and set off after the lady.

The moment the eyes of Emmeline's mother fell upon the countenance of Leopold, whom, notwithstanding the change that suffering had caused, she recognized at once, partly by the peculiarity of his complexion, the suspicion, almost conviction, awoke in her that here was the murderer of her daughter. That he looked so ill seemed only to confirm the likelihood. Her first idea was to wake him and see the effect of her sudden presence. Finding he was attended, however, she hurried away to inquire in the town and discover all she could about him.

A few moments after Polwarth had taken charge of him, and while he stood looking on him tenderly, the youth woke with a start.

"Where is Helen?" he said.

"I have not seen her. Ah, here she comes!"

"Did you find me alone then?"

"Mr. Wingfold was with you. He gave you up to me, because he had to go into the town."

He looked inquiringly at his sister as she came up, and she looked in the same way at Polwarth.

"I feel as if I had been lying all alone in this wide field," said Leopold, "and as if Emmeline had been by me, though I didn't see her."

Polwarth looked after the two retiring forms, which were now almost at the end of the meadow, and about to issue on the high road.

Helen followed his look with hers. A sense of danger seized her. She trembled, and kept behind Leopold's chair.

"Have you been coughing much to-day?" asked the gate-keeper.

"Yes, a good deal—before I came out. But it does not seem to do much good."

"What good would you have it do?"

"I mean, it doesn't do much to get it over. Oh, Mr. Polwarth, I am so tired!"

"Poor fellow! I suppose it looks to you as if it would never be over. But all the millions of the dead have got through it before you. I don't know that that makes much difference to the one who is going through it. And yet it is a sort of company. Only, the Lord of Life is with you, and that is real company, even in dying, when no one else can be with you."

"If I could only feel he was with me!"

"You may feel his presence without knowing what it is."

"I hope it isn't wrong to wish it over, Mr. Polwarth?"

"I don't think it is wrong to wish anything you can talk to him about and submit to his will. St. Paul says, 'In everything let your requests be made known unto God.'"

"I sometimes feel as if I would not ask him for anything, but just let him give me what he likes."

"We must not want to be better than is required of us, for that is at once to grow worse."

"I don't quite understand you."

"Not to ask may seem to you a more submissive way, but I don't think it is so childlike. It seems to me far better to say, 'O Lord, I should like this or that, but I would rather not have it if thou dost not like it also.' Such prayer brings us into conscious and immediate relations with God. Remember, our thoughts are then, passing to him, sent by our will into his mind. Our Lord taught us to pray always and not get tired of it. God, however poor creatures we may be, would have us talk to him, for then he can speak to us better than when we turn no face to him."

"I wonder what I shall do the first thing when I find myself out—out, I mean, in the air, you know."

"It does seem strange we should know so little of what is in some sense so near us! that such a thin veil should be so impenetrable! I fancy the first thing I should do would be to pray."

"Then you think we shall pray there—wherever it is?"

"It seems to me as if I should go up in prayer the moment I got out of this dungeon of a body. I am wrong to call it a dungeon, for it lies open to God's fair world, and the loveliness of the earth comes into me through eyes and ears just as well as into you. Still it is a pleasant thought that it will drop off me some day. But for prayer—I think all will pray there more than here—in their hearts and souls I mean."

"Then where would be the harm if you were to pray for me after I am gone?"

"Nowhere that I know. It were indeed a strange thing if I might pray for you up to the moment when you ceased to breathe, and therewith an iron gate close between us, and I could not even reach you through the ear of the Father of us both! It is a faithless doctrine, for it supposes either that those parted from us can do without prayer, the thing Jesus himself could not do without, seeing it was his highest joy, or that God has so parted those who are in him from these who are in him, that there is no longer any relation, even with God, common to them. The thing to me takes the form of an absurdity."

"Ah, then, pray for me when I am dying, and don't be careful to stop when you think I am gone, Mr. Polwarth."

"I will remember," said the little man.

And now Helen had recovered herself, and came and took her usual seat by her brother's side. She cast an anxious glance now and then into Polwarth's face, but dared not ask him anything.

CHAPTER XXI.

THE BLOOD-HOUND TRAVERSED.

Emmeline's mother had not gone far before she became aware that she was followed. It was a turning of the tables which she did not relish. As would not have been unnatural, even had she been at peace with all the world, a certain feeling of undefined terror came upon her and threatened to overmaster her. It was the more oppressive that she did not choose to turn and face her pursuer, feeling that to do so would be to confess consciousness of cause. The fate of her daughter, seldom absent from her thoughts, now rose before her in association with herself, and was gradually swelling uneasiness into terror: who could tell but this man pressing on her heels in the solitary meadow, and not the poor youth who lay dying there in the chair, and who might indeed be only another of his victims, was the murderer of Emmeline! Unconsciously she accelerated her pace until it was almost a run, but did not thereby widen by a single yard the distance between her and the curate.

When she came out on the high road, she gave a glance in each direction, and, avoiding the country, made for the houses. A short lane led her into Pine street. There she felt safe, the more that it was market-day and a good many people about, and slackened her pace, feeling confident that her pursuer, whoever he was, would now turn aside. But she was disappointed, for, casting a glance over her shoulder, she saw that he still kept the same distance behind her. She saw also, in that single look, that he was well-known, for several were saluting him at once. What could it mean? It must be the G. B. of the Temple! Should she stop and challenge his pursuit? The obstacle to this was a certain sinking at the heart accounted for by an old memory. She must elude him instead. But she did not know a single person in the place, or one house where she could seek refuge. There was an hotel before her! But, unattended, heated, disordered, to all appearance disreputable, what account could she give of herself? That she had been followed by some one everybody knew, and to whom everybody would listen! Feebly debating thus with herself, she hurried along the pavement of Pine Street, with the Abbey church before her.

The footsteps behind her grew louder and quicker: the man had made up his mind and was coming up with her! He might be mad, or ready to run all risks! Probably he knew his life at stake through her perseverance and determination!

On came the footsteps, for the curate had indeed made up his mind to speak to her, and either remove or certify his apprehensions. Nearer yet and nearer they came. Her courage and strength were giving way together, and she should be at his mercy. She darted into a shop, sank on a chair by the counter, and begged for a glass of water. A young woman ran to fetch it, while Mr. Drew went upstairs for a glass of wine. Returning with it he came from behind the counter, and approached the lady where she sat leaning her head upon it.

Meantime the curate also had entered the shop, and placed himself where he might, unseen by her, await her departure, for he could not speak to her there. He had her full in sight when Mr. Drew went up to her.

"Do me the favour, madam," he said—but said no more. For at the sound of his voice, the lady gave a violent start, and raising her head looked at him. The wine-glass dropped from his hand. She gave a half-choked cry, and sped from the shop.

The curate was on the spring after her when he was arrested by the look of the draper: he stood fixed where she had left him, white and trembling as if he had seen a ghost. He went up to him, and said in a whisper:

"Who is she?"

"Mrs. Drew," answered the draper, and the curate was after her like a greyhound.

A little crowd of the shop-people gathered in consternation about their master.

"Pick up those pieces of glass, and call Jacob to wipe the floor," he said—then walked to the door, and stood staring after the curate as he all but ran to overtake the swiftly gliding figure.

The woman, ignorant that her pursuer was again upon her track, and hardly any longer knowing what she did, hurried blindly towards the churchyard. Presently the curate relaxed his speed, hoping she would enter it, when he would have her in a fit place for the interview upon which he was, if possible, more determined than ever, now that he had gained, so unexpectedly, such an absolute hold of her. "She must be Emmeline's mother," he said to himself, "—fit mother for such a daughter." The moment he caught sight of the visage lifted from its regard of the sleeping youth, he had suspected the fact. He had not had time to analyze its expression, but there was something dreadful in it. A bold question would determine the suspicion.

She entered the churchyard, saw the Abbey door open, and hastened to it. She was in a state of bewilderment and terror that would have crazed a weaker woman. In the porch she cast a glance behind her: there again was her pursuer! She sprang into the church. A woman was dusting a pew not far from the door.

"Who is that coming?" she asked, in a tone and with a mien that appalled Mrs. Jenkins. She had but to stretch her neck a little to see through the porch.

"Why, it be only the parson, ma'am!" she answered.

"Then I shall hide myself, over there, and you must tell him I went out by that other door. Here's a sovereign for you."

"I thank you, ma'am," said Mrs. Jenkins, looking wistfully at the sovereign, which was a great sum of money to a sexton's wife with children, then instantly going on with her dusting; "but it ain't no use tryin' of tricks with our parson. HE ain't one of your Mollies. A man as don't play no tricks with hisself, as I heerd a gentleman say, it ain't no use tryin' no tricks with HIM."

Almost while she spoke, the curate entered. The suppliant drew herself up, and endeavoured to look both dignified and injured.

"Would you oblige me by walking this way for a moment?" he said, coming straight to her.

Without a word she followed him, a long way up the church, to the stone screen which divided the chancel from the nave. There, in sight of Mrs. Jenkins, but so far off that she could not hear a word said, he asked her to take a seat on the steps that led up to the door in the centre of the screen. Again she obeyed, and Wingfold sat down near her.

"Are you Emmeline's mother?" he said.

The gasp, the expression of eye and cheek, the whole startled response of the woman, revealed that he had struck the truth. But she made no answer.

"You had better be open with me," he said, "for I mean to be very open with you."

She stared at him, but either could not, or would not speak. Probably it was caution: she must hear more.

The curate was already excited, and I fear now got a little angry, for the woman was not pleasant to his eyes.

"I want to tell you," he said, "that the poor youth whom your daughter's behaviour made a murderer of,—"

She gave a cry, and turned like ashes. The curate was ashamed of himself.

"It seems cruel," he said, "but it is the truth. I say he is now dying—will be gone after her in a few weeks. The same blow killed both, only one has taken longer to die. No end can be served by bringing him to justice. Indeed if he were arrested, he would but die on the way to prison. I have followed you to persuade you, if I can, to leave him to his fate and not urge it on. If ever man was sorry, or suffered for his crime,—"

"And pray what is that to me, sir?" cried the avenging mother, who, finding herself entreated, straightway became arrogant. "Will it give me back my child? The villain took her precious life without giving her a moment to prepare for eternity, and you ask me—her mother—to let him go free! I will not. I have vowed vengeance, and I will have it."

"Allow me to say that if you die in that spirit, you will be far worse prepared for eternity than I trust your poor daughter was."

"What is that to you? If I choose to run the risk, it is my business. I tell you it shall not be my fault if the wretch is not brought to the gallows."

"But he cannot live to reach it. The necessary preliminaries would waste all that is left of his life. I only ask of you to let him die in what peace is possible to him. We must forgive our enemies, you know. But indeed he is no enemy of yours."

"No enemy of mine! The man who murdered my child no enemy of mine! I am his enemy then, and that he shall find. If I cannot bring him to the gallows, I can at least make every man and woman in the country point the finger of scorn and hatred at him. I can bring him and all his to disgrace and ruin. Their pride indeed! They were far too grand to visit me, but not to send a murderer into my family. I am in my rights, and I will have justice. We shall see if they are too grand to have a nephew hung! My poor lovely innocent! I will have justice on the foul villain. Cringing shall not turn me."

Her lips were white, and her teeth set. She rose with the slow movement of one whose intent, if it had blossomed in passion, was yet rooted in determination, and turned to leave the church.

"It might hamper your proceedings a little," said Wingfold, "if in the meantime a charge of bigamy were brought against yourself, MRS. DREW!"

Her back was towards the curate, and for a moment she stood like another pillar of salt. Then she began to tremble, and laid hold of the carved top of a bench. But her strength failed her completely; she sank on her knees and fell on the floor with a deep moan.

The curate called Mrs. Jenkins and sent her for water. With some difficulty they brought her to herself.

She rose, shuddered, drew her shawl about her, and said to the woman,

"I am sorry to give so much trouble. When does the next train start for London?"

"Within an hour," answered the curate. "I will see you safe to it."

"Excuse me; I prefer going alone."

"That I cannot permit."

"I must go to my lodgings first."

"I will go with you."

She cast on him a look of questioning hate, yielded, and laid two fingers on his offered arm.

They walked out of the church together and to the cottage where, for privacy, she had lodged. There he left her for half an hour, and, yielding to her own necessities and not his entreaties, she took some refreshment. In the glowing sullenness of foiled revenge, the smoke of which was crossed every now and then by a flash of hate, she sat until he returned.

"Before I go with you to the train," said the curate, re-entering, "you must give me your word to leave young Lingard unmolested. I know my friend Mr. Drew has no desire to trouble you, but I am equally confident that he will do whatever I ask him. If you will not promise me, from the moment you get into the train you shall be watched.—Do you promise?"

She was silent, with cold gleaming eyes, for a time, then said,

"How am I to know that this is not a trick to save his life?"

"You saw him; you could see he is dying. I tell you I do not think he can live a month. His disease is making rapid progress. He must go with the first of the cold weather."

She could not help believing him.

"I promise," she said. "But you are cruel to compel a mother to forgive the villain that stabbed her daughter to the heart."

"If the poor lad were not dying, I should see that he gave himself up, as indeed he set out to do some weeks ago, but was frustrated by his friends. He is dying for love of her. I believe I say so with truth. Pity and love and remorse and horror of his deed have brought him to the state you saw him in. To be honest with you, he might have got better enough to be tortured for a while in a madhouse, for no jury would have brought him in anything but insane at the time, with the evidence that would have been adduced; but in his anxiety to see me one day—for his friends at that time did not favour my visits, because I encouraged him to surrender—he got out of the house alone to come to me, but fainted in the churchyard, and lay on the damp earth for the better part of an hour, I fancy, before we found him. Still, had it not been for the state of his mind, he might have got over that too.—As you hope to be forgiven, you must forgive him."

He held out his hand to her. She was a little softened, and gave him hers.

"Allow me one word more," said the curate, "and then we shall go: Our crimes are friends that will hunt us either to the bosom of God, or the pit of hell."

She looked down, but her look was still sullen and proud.

The curate rose, took up her bag, went with her to the station, got her ticket, and saw her off.

Then he hastened back to Drew, and told him the whole story.

"Poor woman!" said her husband. "—But God only knows how much *I* am to blame for all this. If I had behaved better to her she might never have left me, and your poor young friend would now be well and happy."

"Perhaps consuming his soul to a cinder with that odious drug," said Wingfold. "'Tis true, as Edgar in King Lear says:

The gods are just,
and of our pleasant vices
Make instruments to plague us;

but he takes our sins on himself, and while he drives them out of us with a whip of scorpions he will yet make them work his ends. He defeats our sins, makes them prisoners, forces them into the service of good, chains them like galley-slaves to the rowing-benches of the gospel-ship, or sets them like ugly gurgoyles or corbels or brackets in the walls of his temples.—No, that last figure I retract. I don't like it. It implies their continuance."

"Poor woman!" said Mr. Drew again, who for once had been inattentive to the curate. "Well! she is sorely punished too."

"She will be worse punished yet," said the curate, "if I can read the signs of character. SHE is not repentant yet—though I did spy in her just once a touch of softening."

"It is an awful retribution," said the draper, "and I may yet have to bear my share—God help me!"

"I suspect it is the weight of her own crime that makes her so fierce to avenge her daughter. I doubt if anything makes one so unforgiving as guilt unrepented of."

"Well, I must try to find out where she is, and keep an eye upon her."

"That will be easy enough. But why?"

"Because, if, as you think, there is more evil in store for her, I may yet have it in my power to do her some service.—I wonder if Mr. Polwarth would call that DIVINE SERVICE," he added, with one of his sunny smiles.

"Indeed he would," answered the curate.

CHAPTER XXII.

THE BEDSIDE.

George Bascombe, when he went to Paris, had no thought of deserting Helen. But he had good ground for fearing that it might be ruinous both to Lingard and himself to undertake his defence. From Paris he wrote often to Helen, and she replied—not so often, yet often enough to satisfy him; and as soon as she was convinced that Leopold could not recover, she let him know, whereupon he instantly began his preparations for returning.

Before he came, the weather had changed once more. It was now cold, and the cold had begun at once to tell upon the invalid. There are some natures to which cold, moral, spiritual, or physical, is lethal, and Lingard's was of the class. When the dying leaves began to shiver in the breath of the coming winter, the very brightness of the sun to look gleamy, and nature to put on the unfriendly aspect of a world not made for living in but for shutting out—when all things took the turn of reminding man that his life lay not in them, Leopold began to shrink and withdraw. He could not face the ghastly persistence of the winter, which would come, let all the souls of the summer-nations shrink and protest as they might; let them creep shivering to Hades; he would have his day.

His sufferings were now considerable, but he never complained. Restless and fevered and sick at heart, it was yet more from the necessity of a lovely nature than from any virtue of will that he was so easy to nurse, accepting so readily all ministrations. Never exacting and never refusing, he was always gently grateful, giving a sort of impression that he could have been far more thankful had he not known the object of the kindnesses so unworthy. Next to Wingfold's and his sister's, the face he always welcomed most was that of the gate-keeper—indeed I ought hardly to say NEXT to theirs; for if the curate was to him as a brother, Polwarth was like a father in Christ. He came every day, and every day, almost till that of his departure, Leopold had something to ask him about or something to tell him.

"I am getting so stupid, Mr. Polwarth!" he said once. "It troubles me much. I don't seem to care for anything now. I don't want to hear the New Testament: I would rather hear a child's story—something that did not want thinking about. If I am not coughing, I am content. I could lie for hours and hours and never think more than what goes creeping through my mind no faster than a canal in Holland. When I am coughing,—I don't think about anything then either—only long for the fit to be over and let me back again into Sleepy Hollow. All my past life seems to be gone from me. I don't care about it. Even my crime looks like something done ages ago. I know it is mine, and I would rather it were not mine, but it is as if a great cloud had come and swept away the world in which it took place. I am afraid sometimes that I am beginning not to care even about that. I say to myself, I shall be sorry again by and by, but I can't think about it now. I feel as if I had handed it over to God to lay down where I should find it again when I was able to think and be sorry."

This was a long utterance for him to make, but he had spoken slowly, and with frequent pauses. Polwarth did not speak once, feeling that a dying man must be allowed to ease his mind after his own fashion, and take as much time to it as he pleased. Helen and Wingfold both would have told him he must not tire himself, but that Polwarth never did. The dying should not have their utterances checked, or the feeling of not having finished forced upon them. They will always have plenty of the feeling without that.

A fit of coughing compelled him to break off, and when it was over, he lay panting and weary, but with his large eyes questioning the face of Polwarth. Then the little man spoke.

"He must give us every sort of opportunity for trusting him," he said. "The one he now gives you, is this dulness that has come over you. Trust him through it, submitting to it and yet trusting against it, and you get the good of it. In your present state perhaps you cannot even try to bring about by force of will any better state of feeling or higher intellectual condition; but you can say to God something like this: "See, Lord, I am dull and stupid, and care for nothing: take thou care of everything for me, heart and mind and all. I leave all to thee. Wilt thou not at length draw me out of this my frozen wintery state? Let me not shrink from fresh life and thought and duty, or be unready to come out of the shell of my sickness when thou sendest for me. I wait thy will. I wait even the light that I feel now as if I dared not encounter for weariness of body and faintness of spirit."

"Ah!" cried Leopold, "there you have touched it! How can you know so well what I feel?"

"Because I have often had to fight hard to keep death to his own province, and not let him cross over into my spirit."

"Alas! I am not fighting at all; I am only letting things go."

"You are fighting more than you know, I suspect, for you are enduring, and that patiently. Suppose Jesus were to knock at the door now, and it was locked; suppose you knew it was he, and there was no one in the room to open it for him; suppose you were as weak as you are now, and seemed to care as little about him or anything else: what would you do?"

Leopold looked half amazed, as if wondering what his friend could be driving at with such a question.

"What else could I do but get up and open it?" he said.

"Would you not be tempted to lie still and wait till some one came."

"No."

"Would you not say in your heart, 'The Lord knows I am very weak, and I should catch cold, and the exertion would make me cough dreadfully, and he won't mind if I lie still?'"

"That I wouldn't! What should I care what came to me? What would it matter so long as I got one look at him! Besides, if he didn't want me to get up, he wouldn't knock."

"But suppose you knew that the moment you turned the key you would drop down, and when the Lord came in you would not see him."

"I can't think where you want to take me, Mr. Polwarth!" said the youth. "Even if I knew I should drop dead the moment I got out on the floor, what would it matter! I should get to him the sooner then, and tell him why I didn't open the door. Can you suppose for a moment I should let any care for this miserable body of mine come between my eyes and the face of my Lord?"

"You see then that you do care about him a little, though a minute ago you didn't think it! There are many feelings in us that are not able to get up stairs the moment we call them. Be as dull and stupid as it pleases God to let you be, and trouble neither yourself nor him about that, only ask him to be with you all the same."

The little man dropped on his knees by the bedside, and said,

"O Lord Jesus, be near when it seems to us, as it seemed to thee once, that our Father has forsaken us, and gathered back to himself all the gifts he once gave us. Even thou who wast mighty in death, didst need the presence of thy Father to make thee able to endure: forget not us the work of thy hands, yea, the labour of thy heart and spirit. O remember that we are his offspring, neither accountable for our own being, nor able to comfort or strengthen ourselves. If thou wert to leave us alone, we should cry out upon thee as on the mother who threw her babes to the wolves—and there are no wolves able to terrify thee. Ah Lord! we know thou leavest us not, only in our weakness we would comfort our hearts with the music of the words of faith. Thou canst not do other than care for us, Lord Christ, for whether we be glad or sorry, slow of heart or full of faith, all the same are we the children of thy Father. He sent us here, and never asked us if we would; therefore thou must be with us, and give us repentance and humility and love and faith, that we may indeed be the children of thy Father who is in heaven. Amen."

While Polwarth was yet praying, the door had opened gently behind him, and Helen, not knowing that he was there, had entered with Bascombe. He neither heard their entrance, nor saw the face of disgust that George made behind his back. What was in Bascombe's deepest soul who shall tell? Of that region he himself knew nothing. It was a silent, holy place into which he had never yet entered— therefore lonely and deserted as the top of Sinai after the cloud had departed. No—I will not say that: who knows what is where man cannot or will not look? If George had sought there, perhaps he might have found traces of a presence not yet altogether vanished. In what he called and imagined his deeepest soul, however, all he was now conscious of was a perfect loathing of the monstrous superstition so fitly embodied before him. The prayer of the kneeling absurdity was to him an audacious mockery of the infrangible laws of Nature: this hulk of misshapen pottery actually presuming to believe that an invisible individual heard what he said because he crooked his hinges to say it! It did not occur to George that the infrangible laws of Nature she had herself from the very first so agonizingly broken to the poor dwarf, she had been to him such a cruel step-mother, that he was in evil case indeed if he could find no father to give him fair play and a chance of the endurable. Was he so much to blame if he felt the annihilation offered by such theorists as George, not altogether a satisfactory counterpoise either to its existence or its loss? If, even, he were to fancy in his trouble that the old fable of an elder brother, something more humble than grand handsome George Bascombe and more ready to help his little brothers and sisters, might be true, seeing that an old story is not necessarily a false one, and were to try after the hints it gave, surely in his condition such folly, however absurd to a man of George Bascombe's endowments, might of the more gifted ephemeros be pardoned if not pitied. Nor will I assert that he was altogether unaware of any admixture of the sad with the ludicrous when he saw the amorphous agglomerate of human shreds and patches kneeling by the bedside of the dying murderer, to pray some comfort into his passing soul. But his "gorge rose at the nonsense and stuff of it," while through Helen ran a cold shudder of disgust at the familiarity and irreverence of the little spiritual prig.

How many of the judgments we are told not to judge and yet do judge, must make the angels of the judging and the judged turn and look at each other and smile a sad smile, ere they set themselves to forget that which so sorely needs to be forgotten.

Polwarth rose from his knees unaware of a hostile presence.

"Leopold," he said, taking his hand, "I would gladly, if I might, walk with you through the shadow. But the heart of all hearts will be with you. Rest in your tent a little while, which is indeed the hollow of the Father's hand turned over you, with your strong brother watching the door. Your imagination cannot go beyond the truth of him who is the Father of lights, or of him who is the Elder Brother of men."

Leopold answered only with his eyes. Polwarth turned to go, and saw the on-lookers. They stood between him and the door, but parted and made room for him to pass. Neither spoke. He made a bow first to one and then to the other, looking up in the face of each, unabashed by smile or scorn or blush of annoyance, but George took no notice, walking straight to the bed the moment the way was clear. Helen's conscience, however, or heart, smote her, and, returning his bow, she opened the door for her brother's friend. He thanked her, and went his way.

"Poor dear fellow!" said George kindly, and stroked the thin hand laid in his: "can I do anything for you?"

"Nothing but be good to Helen when I am gone, and tell her now and then that I'm not dead, but living in the hope of seeing her again one day before long. She might forget sometimes—not me, but that, you know."

"Yes, yes, I'll see to it," answered George, in the evil tone of one who faithfully promises a child an impossibility. Of course there was no more harm in lying to a man who was just on the verge of being a man no more, and becoming only an unpleasant mass of chemicals, which a whole ant-heap of little laws would presently be carrying outside the gates of the organic, than there had been in lying to him when he supposed him a madman. Neither could anyone blame him for inconsistency; for had he not always said in the goodness of his heart, that he would never disturb the faith of old people drawing nigh their end, because such no more possessed the needful elasticity of brain to accommodate themselves to the subversion of previous modes of feeling and thought, unavoidable to the adoption of his precious revelation. Precious he did believe it, never having himself one of those visions of infinite hope, which, were his theory once proved as true as he imagined it, must then indeed vanish for ever.

"Do you suffer much?" asked George.

"Yes—a good deal."

"Pain?"

"Not so much;—sometimes. The weakness is the worst. But it doesn't matter: God is with me."

"What good does that do you?" asked George, forgetting himself, half in contempt, half in a curiosity which he would have called, and which perhaps was, scientific.

But Leopold took it in good faith, and answered,

"It sets it all right, and makes me able to be patient."

George laid down the hand he held, and turned sadly to Helen, but said nothing.

The next moment Wingfold entered. Helen kissed the dying hand, and left the room with George.

CHAPTER XXIII.

THE GARDEN.

Tenderly he led her into the garden, and down the walks now bare of bordering flowers. To Helen it looked like a graveyard; the dry bushes were the memorials of the buried flowers, and the cypress and box trees rose like the larger monuments of shapely stone. The day was a cold leaden one, that would have rained if it could, to get rid of the deadness at its heart, but no tears came. To the summer-house they went, under the cedar, and sat down. Neither spoke for some time.

"Poor Leopold!" said George at length, and took Helen's hand.

She burst into tears, and again for some time neither spoke.

"George, I can't bear it!" she said at length.

"It is very sad," answered George. "But he had a happy life, I don't doubt, up to—to—"

"What does that matter now? It is all a horrible farce.—To begin so fair and lovely, and end so stormy and cold and miserable!"

George did not like to say what he thought, namely, that it was Leopold's own doing. He did not see that therein lay the deepest depth of the misery—the thing that of all things needed help: all else might be borne; the less that COULD be borne the better.

"It IS horrible," he said. "But what can be done? What's done is done, and nobody can help it."

"There should be somebody to help it," said Helen.

"Ah! Should be!" said George. "—Well, it's a comfort it will soon be over!"

"Is it?" returned Helen almost sharply. "—But he's not your brother, and you don't know what it is to lose him! Oh, how desolate the world will be without my darling!"

And again her tears found way.

"All that I can do to make up for the loss, dearest Helen," said George,—

"Oh George!" she cried, starting to her feet, "is there NO hope? I don't mean of his getting better—that we do know the likelihoods of—but is there no hope of SOME TIME seeing him again? We know so little about all of it! MIGHT there not be some way?"

But George was too honest in himself, and too true to his principles, to pretend anything to Helen. Hers was an altogether different case from Leopold's. Here was a young woman full of health and life and hope, with all her joys before her! Many suns must set before her sun would go down, many pale moons look lovely in her eyes, ere came those that would mock her with withered memories—a whole hortus siccus of passion-flowers. Why should he lie to HER of a hope beyond the grave? Let the pleasures of the world be the dearer to her for the knowledge that they must so soon depart; let love be the sweeter for the mournful thought that it is a thing of the summer, and that when the winter comes it shall be no more! But perhaps George forgot one point. I will allow that the insects of a day, dying in a moment of delightful fruition, are blessed; but when the delicate Psyche, with her jewel-feathered wings, is beat about by a wind full of rain until she lies draggled in the dirt; when there are no more flowers, or if there be, the joy of her hovering is over, and yet death comes but slowly; when the mourners are going about the streets ere ever the silver cord is loosed; when the past looks a mockery and the future a blank;—then perhaps, even to the correlatives of the most triumphant natural selection, it may not merely seem as if something were wrong somewhere, but even as if there ought to be somebody to set wrong right. If Psyche should be so subdued to circumstance as to accept without question her supposed fate, then doubly woe for Psyche!

But if George could not lie, it was not necessary for him to speak the truth: silence was enough. A moment of it was all Helen could endure. She rose hastily, left the wintered summer-house, and walked back to the sick-chamber. George followed a few paces behind, so far quenched that he did not overtake her to walk by her side, feeling he had no aid to offer her. Doubtless he could have told her of help at hand, but it was help that must come, that could neither be given nor taken, would not come the sooner for any prayer, and indeed would not begin to exist until the worst should be over: the nearest George came to belief in a saving power, was to console himself with the thought that TIME would do everything for Helen.

CHAPTER XXIV.

THE DEPARTURE.

As Leopold slowly departed, he seemed to his sister to draw along with him all that was precious in her life. She felt herself grow dull and indifferent. It was to no purpose that she upbraided herself with heartlessness; seemingly heartless her bosom remained. It was not that her mind was occupied with anything else than her brother, or drew comfort from another source; her feelings appeared to be dying with him who had drawn them forth more than any other. The battle was ending without even the poor pomp and circumstance of torn banners and wailful music.

Leopold said very little during the last few days. His fits, of coughing were more frequent, and in the pauses he had neither strength nor desire to speak. When Helen came to his bedside, he would put out his hand to her, and she would sit down by him and hold it warm in hers. The hand of his sister was the point of the planet from which, like his mount of ascension, the spirit of the youth took its departure;—when he let that go, he was gone. But he died asleep, as so many do; and fancied, I presume, that he was waking into his old life, when he woke into his new one.

Wingfold stood on the other side of the bed, with Polwarth by him, for so had the departing wished it, and although he made no sign, I cannot but think he reaped some content therefrom. While yet he lingered, one of Helen's listless, straying glances was arrested by the countenance of the gate-keeper. It was so still and so rapt that she thought he must be seeing within the veil, and regarding what things were awaiting her brother on the reverse of the two-sided wonder. But it was not so. Polwarth saw no more than she did: he was ONLY standing in the presence of him who is not the God of the dead but of the living. Whatever lay in that Will was the life of whatever came of that Will, that is, of every creature, and no to that Will, to the face of the Father, he lifted, in his prayerful thought, the heart and mind and body of the youth now passing through the birth of death. "I know not," he would have said, had he been questioned concerning his spiritual attitude, "how my prayer should for another work anything with the perfect Giver, but at least I will not leave my friend behind when I go into the presence of his Father and my Father. And I believe there is something in it I cannot yet see."

Wingfold's anxiety was all for Helen. He could do no more for Leopold, nor did he need more from man. As to many of the things that puzzled them most, he was on his way to know more; he would soon be in the heart of what seemed likely to remain a long secret to him. But there was his sister, about to be left behind him without his hopes; for her were dreary days at hand; and the curate prayed the God of comfort and consolation to visit her.

Mrs. Ramshorn would now and then look in at the noiseless door of the chamber of death, but she rightly felt her presence was not desired, and though ready to help, did not enter. Neither did George—not from heartlessness, but that he judged it better to leave the priests of falsehood undisturbed in the exercise of their miserable office. What did it matter how many comforting lies were told to a dying man? What COULD it matter? There was small danger of their foolish prayers and superstitious ceremonies evoking a deity from the well-ordered, self-evolved sphericity of interacting law, where not a pin-hole of failure afforded space out of which he might creep. No more could they deprive the poor lad of the bliss of returning into the absolute nothingness whence he had crept—to commit a horrible crime against immortal society, and creep back again, with a heart full of love and remorse and self-abhorrence, into the black abyss. Therefore, why should he not let them tell their lies and utter their silly incantations? Aloof and unharmed he stood, safe on the shore, all ready to reach the rescuing hand to Helen, the moment she should turn her eyes to him, for the help she knew he had to give her. Certainly, for her sake, he would rather she were not left unprotected to such subtle and insinuating influences; but with the power of his mind upon her good sense, he had no fear of the result. Not that he expected her to submit at once to the wholesome regimen and plain diet he must prescribe her: the soft hand of Time must first draw together the edges of her heart's wound.

But the deadness of Helen's feelings, the heartlessness because of which she cried out against herself, seemed, in a vague way, by herself unacknowledged yet felt, if not caused by, yet associated with some subtle radiation from the being of George Bascombe. That very morning when he came into the breakfast-room so quietly that she had not heard him, and, looking up, saw him unexpectedly, he seemed for a moment, she could not tell why, the dull fountain of all the miserable feeling—not of loss, but of no loss, which pressed her heart flat in her bosom. The next moment she accused herself of the grossest injustice, attributing it to the sickness of soul which the shadow of death had wrought in her; for was not George the only true friend she had ever had? If she lost him she must be lonely indeed!—The feeling lingered notwithstanding, and when she thought it dispelled, began to gather again immediately.

At the same time she shrunk from Wingfold as hard and unsympathetic. True he had been most kind, even tender, to her brother, but to him he had taken a fancy, having found in him one whom he could work upon and fashion to his own liking: poor Poldie had never been one of the strongest of men. But to her, whom he could not model after his own ideas, who required a reason for the thing anyone would have her believe—to her he had shown the rough side of his nature, going farther than any gentleman ought, even if he was a clergyman, in criticizing her conduct. He might well take example of her cousin George! What a different sort of artillery HE had brought to bear upon the outstanding fortress of her convictions!

So would she say within herself, again and again, in different forms, not knowing how little of conviction there was in the conclusions she seemed to come to—how much of old habit and gratitude on the one hand, and pride and resentment upon the other.-And there still was that feeling! she could not drive it away. It was like trying to disperse a fog with a fan.

The outside weather, although she was far past heeding that, was in harmony with her soul's weather. A dull dark-grey fog hung from the sky, and without much obscuring the earth altogether hid the sun. The air was very cold. There was neither joy nor hope anywhere. The bushes were leafless and budless, the summer gone, the spring not worth hoping for, because it also would go: spring after spring came—for nothing but to go again! Things were so empty and wretched that pain and grief, almost fear itself, would have been welcome. The world around her, yes, all her life, all herself, was but the cold dead body of a summer-world. And Leopold was going to be buried with the summer. His smiles had all gone with the flowers. The weeds of his troubles were going also, for they would die with him. But he would not know it and be glad, any more than she, who was left caring for neither summer nor winter, joy nor sorrow, love nor hate, the past nor the future.

Many such thoughts wandered hazily through her mind as she now sat holding the hand of him who was fast sleeping away from her into death. Her eyes were fixed on the window through which he had entered that terrible night, but she saw nothing beyond it.

"He is gone" said Polwarth in a voice that sounded unknown to the ears of Helen, and as he spoke he kneeled.

She started up with a cry, and looked in her brother's face. She had never seen anyone die, and yet she saw that he was dead.

CHAPTER XXV.

THE SUNSET.

How the terrible time, terrible for its very dulness and insensibility, passed until it brought the funeral, Helen could not have told. It seemed to her, as she looked back upon it, a bare blank, yet was the blank full of a waste weariness of heart. The days were all one, outside and inside. Her heart was but a lonely narrow bay to the sea of cold immovable fog that filled the world. No one tried to help, no one indeed knew her trouble. Everyone took it for grief at the loss of her brother, while to herself it was the oppression of a life that had not even the interest of pain. The curate had of course called to inquire after her, but had not been invited to enter. George had been everywhere with help, but had no word to speak.

The day of the funeral came, in thin fog and dull cold. The few friends gathered. The body was borne to the Abbey. The curate received it at the gate in the name of the church—which takes our children in its arms, and our bodies into its garden—save indeed where her gardener is some foolish priest who knows not the heart of his mother, and will pick and choose among her dead;—the lovely words of the last-first of the apostles, were read; and earth was given back to earth, to mingle with the rest of the stuff the great workman works withal. Cold was Helen's heart, cold her body, cold her very being. The earth, the air, the mist, the very light was cold. The past was cold, the future yet colder. She would have grudged Leopold his lonely rest in the grave, but that she had not feeling enough even for that. Her life seemed withering away from her, like an autumn flower in the frosts of winter; and she, as if she had been but a flower, did not seem to care. What was life worth, when it had not strength to desire even its own continuance? Heartless she returned from the grave, careless of George's mute attentions, not even scornful of her aunt's shallow wail over the uncertainty of life and all things human,—so indifferent to the whole misery that she walked straight up to the room, hers once more, from which the body had just been carried, and which, for so many many weary weeks, had been the centre of loving pain, sometimes agony. Once more she was at peace—but what a peace!

She took off her cloak and bonnet, laid them on the bed, went to the window, sat down, and gazed, hardly seeing, out on the cold garden with its sodden earth, its leafless shrubs, and perennial trees of darkness and mourning. The meadow lay beyond, and there she did see the red cow busily feeding, and was half-angry with her. Beyond the meadow stood the trees, with the park behind them. And yet further behind lay the hollow with the awful house in its bosom, its dismal haunted lake and its ruined garden. But nothing moved her. She could have walked over every room in that house without a single quaver of the praecordia. Poldie was dead, but was it not well? Even if he had not been in trouble, what should his death matter? She would die soon herself and for ever: what did that or anything else matter? Might she but keep this dulness of spirit, and never more wake to weep foolish tears over an existence the whole upstanding broad-based fact of which was not worth one drop in the rivers of weeping that had been flowing ever since the joyless birth of this unconceived, ill-fated, unfathered world! To the hour of death belonged jubilation and not mourning; the hour of birth was the hour of sorrow. Back to the darkness! was the cry of a life whose very being was an injury, only there was no one to have done the injury.

Thus she sat until she was summoned to dinner—early for the sake of the friends whose home lay at a distance. She ate and drank and took her share in the talk as matter of course, believing all at the table would judge her a heartless creature, and careless of what they might think or say. But they judged her more kindly and more truly than she judged herself. They saw through her eyes the deeps whose upward ducts were choked with the frost of an unknown despair.

No sooner was she at liberty than again she sought her room, not consciously from love to her brother who had died there, but because the deadness of her heart chose a fitting loneliness: and again she seated herself at the window.

The dreary day was drawing to a close, and the night, drearier it could not be, was at hand. The gray had grown darker, and she sat like one waiting for the night like a monster coming to claim its own and swallow her up.

Something—was it an invasion of reviving light? caused her to lift her eyes. Away, sideways from her window, in the west, the mist had cleared a little— somewhere about the sun. Thinner and thinner it grew. No sun came forth: he was already down; but a canopy of faint amber grew visible, stretched above his tomb. It was the stuff of which sad smiles are made, not a thing that belonged to gladness. But only he who has lost his sorrow without regaining his joy, can tell how near sorrow lieth to joy. Who that has known the dull paths of listless no-feeling, would not have his sorrow back with all its attendant agonies?

The pale amber spread, dilute with light, and beneath it lay the gray of the fog, and above it the dark blue of cloud—not of sky. The soul of it was so still, so resigned, so sad, so forsaken, that she who had thought her heart gone from her, suddenly felt its wells were filling, and soon they overflowed. She wept. At what? A colour in the sky! Was there then a God that knew sadness—and was that a banner of grief he hung forth to comfort the sorrowful with sympathy? Or was it but a godless colour which the heart varnished with its own grief? Or if the human heart came from nothing and was sad, why might not the aspects of nature come from nothing and be sad too—wrought in harmony with the unutterable woe of humanity? Then either is man the constructive centre of the world, and its meanings are but his own face looking back upon him from the mirror of his own projected atmosphere, and comfort there is none; or he is not the centre of the world, which yet carries in its forms and colours the aspects of his mind; and then, horror of horrors! is man the one conscious point and object of a vast derision—insentient nature grinning at sentient man! rose or saffron, his sky but mocks and makes mows at him; while he himself is the worst mockery of all, being at once that which mocks and that which not only is mocked but writhes in agony under the mockery. Such as Bascombe reply that they find it not so. I answer—For the best of reasons, that it is not so.

Helen's doubts did not stay her weeping, as doubt generally does; for the sky with its sweet sadness was before her, and deep in her heart a lake of tears, which, now that it had begun to flow, would not be stayed. She knew not why she wept, knew not that it was the sympathy of that pale amber of sad resignation which brought her relief: but she wept and wept, until her heart began to stir, and her tears came cooler and freer.

"Oh Poldie! my own Poldie!" she cried at length, and fell upon her knees—not-to worship the sky—not to pray to Poldie, or even for Poldie—not indeed to pray at all, so far as she knew; yet I doubt if it was merely and only from the impulse of the old childish habit of saying prayers.

But in a moment she grew restless. There was no Poldie! She rose and walked about the room. And he came back to her soul, her desolate brother, clothed, alas! in the rags and tatters of all the unkind and unjust thoughts she had ever had concerning him, and wearing on his face the reflection of her worse deeds. She had stood between him and the only poor remnant of peace, consolation, and hope that it was possible he should have; and it was through the friends whom she had treated with such distance and uncordiality that he did receive it. Then out rushed from the chamber of her memory the vision of the small dark nervous wild-looking Indian boy who gazed at her but for one questioning moment, then shot into her arms and nestled in her bosom. How had she justified that faith? She had received, and sheltered, and shielded him, doubtless, and would have done so with her life, yet, when it came to the test, she had loved herself better than him, and would have doomed him to agony rather than herself to disgrace. Oh Poldie! Poldie! But he could not hear! Never, for evermore, should she utter to him word of sorrow or repentance! never beg his forgiveness, or let him know that now she knew better, and had risen above such weakness and selfishness!

She stopped, and looked sadly from the window. The sky was cloudless overhead, and the amber pall was fainter and clearer over the tomb of the sun. She turned hastily to the bed where lay her cloak and bonnet, put them on with trembling hands, and went out by that same window into the garden. She could not help a shudder as she stood in the dark passage unlocking the door in the sunk fence, but the next minute she was crossing the meadow through the cold frosty twilight air, now clear of its fog, and seeming somehow to comfort, uplift, and strengthen her. The red cow was still feeding there. She stopped and talked to her a little. She seemed one of Poldie's friends, and Poldie had come back to her heart if he might never more to her arms, and she was now on her way to one of his best friends, whom, as more worthy, he had loved even better than her, and whom she had not honoured as they deserved or as he must have desired. To get near them, would be to get nearer to Poldie. At least she would be with those whom he had loved, and who, she did not doubt, still loved him, believing him still alive. She could not go to the curate, but she could go to the Polwarths; no one would blame her for that-except indeed George. But even George should not come between her and what mere show of communion with Poldie was left her! She would keep her freedom—would rather break with George than lose an atom of her liberty! She would be no clay for his hands to mould after his pleasure!

She opened the door in the fence and entered the park, seeming to recover strength with every step she took towards Poldie's friends.

It was almost dark when she stood at the lodge-door and knocked.

CHAPTER XXVI.

AN HONEST SPY.

No one answered Helen's knock. She repeated it, and still no answer came. Her heart might have failed her, but that she heard voices: what if they were talking about Leopold? At length, after knocking four or five times, she heard the step as of a child coming down a stair; but it passed the door. Clearly no one had heard her. She knocked yet again, and immediately it was opened by Rachel. The pleasured surprise that shone up in her face when she saw who it was that stood without, was lovely to see, and Helen, on whose miserable isolation it came like a sunrise of humanity, took no counsel with pride, but, in simple gratitude for the voiceless yet eloquent welcome, bent down and kissed her. The little arms were flung about her neck, and the kiss returned with such a gentle warmth and restrained sweetness as would have satisfied the most fastidious in the matter of salute—to which class, however, Helen did not belong, for she seldom kissed anyone. Then Rachel took her by the hand, and led her into the kitchen, placed a chair for her near the fire, and said,

"I AM sorry there is no fire in the parlour. The gentlemen are in my uncle's room. Oh, Miss Lingard, I do wish you could have heard how they have been talking!"

"Have they been saying anything about my brother?" asked Helen.

"It's all about him," she replied.

"May I ask who the gentlemen are?" said Helen doubtfully.

"Mr. Wingfold and Mr. Drew. They are often here."

"Is it—do you mean Mr. Drew, the draper?"

"Yes. He is one of Mr. Wingfold's best pupils. He brought him to my uncle, and he has come often ever since."

"I never heard that—Mr. Wingfold—took pupils.—I am afraid I do not quite understand you.

"I would have said DISCIPLES," returned Rachel smiling; "but that has grown to feel such a sacred word—as if it belonged only to the Master, that I didn't like to use it. It would say best what I mean though; for there are people in Glaston that are actually mending their ways because of Mr. Wingfold's teaching, and Mr. Drew was the first of them. It is long since such a thing was heard of in the Abbey. It never was in my time."

Helen sighed. She wished it had remained possible for her also to become one of Mr. Wingfold's pupils, but how could she now when she had learned that what he had to teach was at best but a lovely phantasm, sprung of the seething together of the conscience and imagination. George could give account of the whole matter: religion invariably excited the imagination and weakened the conscience;—witness the innumerable tales concerning Jesus invented in the first of the Christian centuries, and about this and that saint in those that followed! Helen's experience in Leopold's case had certainly been different, but the other fact remained. Alas, she could not be a pupil of Mr. Wingfold! She could no longer deceive herself with such comfort. And yet!—COME UNTO ME, AND *I* WILL GIVE YOU REST.

"I do wish I could hear them," she said.

"And why not?" returned Rachel. "There is not one of them would not be glad to see you. I know that."

"I am afraid I should hinder their talk. Would they speak just as freely as if I were not there? Not that I know why they shouldn't," she added; "only the presence of any stranger—"

"You are no stranger to Mr. Wingfold or my uncle," said Rachel, "and I daresay you know Mr. Drew?"

"To tell you the truth, Miss Polwarth, I have not behaved as I should either to your uncle or Mr. Wingfold. I know it now that my brother is gone. They were so good to him! I feel now as if I had been possessed with an evil spirit. I could not bear them to be more to him than I was. Oh, how I should like to hear what they are saying! I feel as if I should get a glimpse of Leopold— almost, if I might. But I couldn't face them all together. I could not go into the room."

Rachel was silent for a moment, thinking. Then she said:

"I'll tell you what then: there's no occasion. Between my uncle's room and mine there's a little closet, where you shall sit and hear every word. Nothing will divide you from them but a few thin old boards."

"That would hardly be honourable though—would it?"

"I will answer for it. I shall tell my uncle afterwards. There may be cases where the motive makes the right or the wrong. It's not as if you were listening to find out secrets. I shall be in the room, and that will be a connecting link, you know: they never turn me out. Come now. We don't know what we may be losing."

The desire to hear Leopold's best friends talk about him was strong in Helen, but her heart misgave her: was it not unbecoming? She would be in terror of discovery all the time. In the middle of the stair, she drew Rachel back and whispered,

"I dare not do it."

"Come on," said Rachel. "Hear what I shall say to them first. After that you shall do as you please."

Evidently, so quick was her response, her thoughts had been going in the same direction as Helen's.

"Thank you for trusting me," she added, as Helen again followed her.

Arrived at the top, the one stood trembling, while the other went into the room.

"Uncle," said Rachel, "I have a friend in the house who is very anxious to hear you and our friends speak your minds to each other, but for reasons does not wish to appear: will you allow my friend to listen without being seen?"

"Is it your wish, Rachel, or are you only conveying the request of another?" asked her uncle.

"It is my wish," answered Rachel. "I really desire it—if you do not mind."

She looked from one to another as she spoke. The curate and the draper indicated a full acquiescence.

"Do you know quite what you are about, Rachel?" asked Polwarth.

"Perfectly, uncle," she answered. "There is no reason why you should not talk as freely as if you were talking only to me. I will put my friend in the closet, and you need never think that anyone is in the house but ourselves."

"Then I have no more to say," returned her uncle with a smile. "Your FRIEND, whoever he or she may be, is heartily welcome."

Rachel rejoined Helen, who had already drawn nearer to the door of the closet, and now seated herself right willingly in its shelter, amidst an atmosphere odorous of apples and herbs. Already the talk was going on just as before. At first each of the talkers did now and then remember there was a listener unseen but found, when the conversation came to a close, that he had for a long time forgotten it.

CHAPTER XXVII.

WHAT HELEN HEARD,

Although satisfied that, after what Rachel had said to the men, there could be no impropriety in her making use of the privilege granted her, Helen felt oddly uncomfortable at first. But soon the fancy came, that she was listening at the door of the other world to catch news of her Leopold, and that made her forget herself and put her at peace. For some time, however, the conversation was absolutely unintelligible to her. She understood the words and phrases, and even some of the sentences, but as she had no clue to their drift, the effort to understand was like attempting to realize the span of a rainbow from a foot or two of it appearing now and then in different parts and vanishing again at once. It was chiefly Polwarth, often Wingfold, and now and then Drew that spoke, Rachel contributing only an occasional word. At length broke something of a dawn over the seeming chaos. The words from which the light that first reached Helen flowed, were the draper's.

"I can't think, for all that," he said, "why, if there be life beyond the grave, and most sincerely I trust there is—I don't see why we should know so little about it. Confess now, Mr. Polwarth!—Mr. Wingfold!" he said appealingly, "—does it not seem strange that, if our dearest friends go on living somewhere else, they should, the moment they cease to breathe, pass away from us utterly—so utterly that from that moment neither hint nor trace nor sign of their existence ever reaches us? Nature, the Bible, God himself says nothing about how they exist or where they are, or why they are so silent— cruelly silent if it be in their power to speak,—therefore, they cannot; and here we are left not only with aching hearts but wavering faith, not knowing whither to turn to escape the stare of the awful blank, that seems in the very intensity of its silence to shout in our ears that we are but dust and return to the dust!"

The gate-keeper and curate interchanged a pleased look of surprise at the draper's eloquence, but Polwarth instantly took up his answer.

"I grant you it would be strange indeed if there were no good reason for it," he said.

"Then do you say," asked Wingfold. "that until we see, discover, or devise some good reason for the darkness that overhangs it, we are at liberty to remain in doubt as to whether there be any life within the cloud?"

"I would say so," answered Polwarth, "were it not that we have the story of Jesus, which, if we accept it, is surely enough to satisfy us both as to the thing itself, and as to the existence of a good reason, whether we have found one or not, for the mystery that overshadows it."

"Still I presume we are not forbidden to seek such a reason," said the curate.

The draper was glancing from the one to the other with evident anxiety.

"Certainly not," returned the gate-keeper. "For what else is our imagination given us but the discovery of good reasons that are, or the invention of good reasons that may perhaps be?"

"Can you then imagine any good reason," said Drew, "why we should be kept in such absolute ignorance of everything that befalls the parted spirit from the moment it quits its house with us?"

"I think I know one," answered Polwarth. "I have sometimes fancied it might be because no true idea of their condition could possibly be grasped by those who remain in the tabernacle of the body; that to know their state it is necessary that we also should be clothed in our new bodies, which are to the old as a house to a tent. I doubt if we have any words in which the new facts could be imparted to our knowledge, the facts themselves being beyond the reach of any senses whereof we are now in actual possession. I expect to find my new body provided with new, I mean OTHER senses beyond what I now possess: many more may be required to bring us into relation with all the facts in himself which God may have shadowed forth in properties, as we say, of what we call matter. The spaces all around us, even to those betwixt star and star, may be the home of the multitudes of the heavenly host, yet seemingly empty to all who have but our provision of senses. But I do not care to dwell upon that kind of speculation. It belongs to a lower region, upon which I grudge to expend interest while the far loftier one invites me, where, if I gather not the special barley of which I am in search, I am sure to come upon the finest of wheat.—Well, then, for my reason: There are a thousand individual events in the course of every man's life, by which God takes a hold of him—a thousand breaches by which he would and does enter, little as the man may know it; but there is one universal and unchanging grasp he keeps upon the race, yet not as the race, for the grasp is upon every solitary single individual that has a part in it: that grasp is—death in its mystery. To whom can the man who is about to die in absolute loneliness and go he cannot tell whither, flee for refuge from the doubts and fears that assail him, but to the Father of his being?"

"But," said Drew, "I cannot see what harm would come of letting us know a little—as much at least as might serve to assure us that there was more of SOMETHING on the other side."

"Just this," returned Polwarth, "that, their fears allayed, their hopes encouraged from any lower quarter, men would, as usual, turn away from the fountain to the cistern of life, from the ever fresh original creative Love to that drawn off and shut in. That there are thousands who would forget God if they could but be assured of such a tolerable state of things beyond the grave as even this wherein we now live, is plainly to be anticipated from the fact that the doubts of so many in respect of religion concentrate themselves now-a-days upon the question whether there is any life beyond the grave; a question which, although no doubt nearly associated with religion,—as what question worth asking is not?—does not immediately belong to religion at all. Satisfy such people, if you can, that they shall live, and what have they gained? A little comfort perhaps—but a comfort not from the highest source, and possibly gained too soon for their well-being. Does it bring them any nearer to God than they were before? Is he filling one cranny more of their hearts in consequence? Their assurance of immortality has not come from a knowledge of him, and without him it is worse than worthless. Little indeed has been gained, and that with the loss of much. The word applies here which our Lord in his parable puts into the mouth of Abraham: If they hear not Moses and the prophets, neither will they be persuaded though one rose from the dead. He does not say they would not believe in a future state though one rose from the dead—although most likely they would soon persuade themselves that the apparition after all was only an illusion—[Footnote: See Lynch's admirable sermon on this subject.] but that they would not be persuaded to repent, though one rose from the dead; and without that, what great matter whether they believed in a future state or not? It would only be the worse for them if they did. No, Mr. Drew! I repeat, it is not a belief in immortality that will deliver a man from the woes of humanity, but faith in the God of life, the father of lights, the God of all consolation and comfort. Believing in him, a man can leave his friends, and their and his own immortality, with everything else—even his and their love and perfection, with utter confidence in his hands. Until we have the life in us, we shall never be at peace. The living God dwelling in the heart he has made, and glorifying it by inmost speech with himself—that is life, assurance, and safety. Nothing less is or can be such."

CHAPTER XXVIII.

WHAT HELEN HEARD MORE

"A word you dropped the other day," said the curate, "set me thinking of the note-worthy fact that belief in God and belief in immortality cease together. But I do not see the logic of it. If we are here without God, why may we not go on there without God? I marvel that I have heard of no one taking up and advocating the view. What a grand discovery it would be for some people—that not only was there no God to interfere with them, and insist on their becoming something worth being, but that they were immortal notwithstanding! that death was only the passage of another birth into a condition of enlarged capacity for such bliss as they enjoyed here, but more exalted in degree, perhaps in kind, and altogether preferable."

"I know one to whom the thought would not have been a new one," said Polwarth. "Have you not come upon a passage in my brother's manuscript involving the very idea?"

"Not yet. I read very slowly and pick up all the crumbs. I wish we had had the book here. I should have so much liked to hear you read from it again."

The gate-keeper rose and went to his cabinet.

"The wish is easily gratified," he said. "I made a copy of it,—partly for security, partly that I might thoroughly enter into my brother's thoughts."

"I wonder almost you lend the original then," said Wingfold.

"I certainly could not lend the copy to any man I could not trust with the original," answered Polwarth. "But I never lent either before."—He was turning over the leaves as he spoke.—"The passage," he went on, "besides for its own worth, is precious to me as showing how, through all his madness, his thoughts haunted the gates of wisdom.—Ah! here it is!

"'About this time I had another strange vision, whether in the body or out of the body, I cannot tell. I thought, as oftener than once before, that at length I was dying. And it seemed to me that I did die, and awake to the consciousness of a blessed freedom from the coarser and more ponderous outer dress I had hitherto worn, being now clad only in what had been up to this time an inner garment, and was a far more closely fitting one. The first delight of which I was aware was coolness—a coolness that hurt me not—the coolness as of a dewy summer eve, in which a soft friendly wind is blowing; and the coolness was that of perfect well-being, of the health that cometh after fever, when a sound sleep hath divided it away and built a rampart between; the coolness of undoubted truth, and of love that has surmounted passion and is tenfold love.'

"He goes on to give further and fuller account of his sensations,—ventures even on the anticipated futility of an attempt to convey a notion of one of his new senses. I leave all that for your own reading, Mr. Wingfold.

"'But where was I? That I could not tell. I am here was all I could say; but then what more could I ever have said?—Gradually my sight came to me, or the light of the country arose, I could not tell which, and behold, I was in the midst of a paradise, gorgeous yet gracious, to describe which I find no words in the halting tongues of earth, and I know something of them all, most of them well. If I say a purple sea was breaking in light on an emerald shore, the moment the words are written, I see them coarse and crude as a boy's first attempt at landscape; yet are there no better wherewith to tell what first filled my eyes with heavenly delight.

"'The inhabitants were many, but nowhere were they crowded. There was room in abundance, and wild places seemed to be held sacred for solitude.'

"I am only picking up a sentence here and there, as I hasten to the particular point," said Polwarth, looking down the page.

"'But the flowers! and the birds! and above all the beauty of the people! And they dwelt in harmony. Yet on their foreheads lay as it seemed a faint mist, or as it were the first of a cloud of coming disquiet.

"'And I prayed him, Tell me, sir, whither shall I go to find God and say unto him, Lo, here I am! And he answered and said to me, Sir, I but dimly know what thou meanest. Say further. And I stood for an hour, even as one astonied. Then said I, All my long life on the world whence I came, I did look to find God when death should take me. But lo, now—And with that my heart smote me, for in my former life I had oftentimes fallen into unbelief and denied God: was this now my punishment—that I should never find him? And my heart grew cold in my body, and the blood curdled therein. Then the man answered and said, It is true that in generations past, for so I read in our ancient books, men did believe in one above them and in them, who had wrought them to that they were, and was working them to better still; but whether it be that we have now gained that better, and there is nothing higher unto which we may look, therefore no need of the high one, I know not, but truly we have long ceased so to believe, and have learned that, as things are, so they have been, and so they shall be. Then fell as it were a cold stone into the core of my heart, and I questioned him no farther, for I bore death in my heart, even as a woman carrieth her unborn child. No God! I cried, and sped away into a solitude and shrieked aloud, No God! Nay, but ere I believe it, I will search through all creation, and cry aloud as I go. I will search until I find him, and if I find him not,—. With that my soul would have fainted in me, had I not spread forth my wings and rushed aloft to find him.

"'For the more lovely anything I saw, the more gracious in colour or form, or the more marvellous in the law of its working, ever a fresh pang shot to my heart: if that which I had heard should prove true, then was there no Love such as seemed to me to dwell therein, the soul of its beauty, and all the excellence thereof was but a delusion of my own heart, greedy after a phantom perfection. No God! no Love! no loveliness, save a ghastly semblance thereof! and the more ghastly that it was so like loveliness, and yet was not to be loved upon peril of prostitution of spirit. Then in truth was heaven a fable, and hell an all-embracing fact! for my very being knew in itself that if it would dwell in peace, the very atmosphere in which it lived and moved and breathed must be love, living love, a one divine presence, truth to itself, and love to me, and to all them that needed love, down to the poorest that can but need it, and knoweth it not when it cometh. I knew that if love was not all in all, in fact as well as in imagination, my life was but a dreary hollow made in the shape of a life, and therefore for ever hungry and never to be satisfied. And again I spread wings—no longer as it seemed of hope, but wings of despair, yet mighty, and flew. And I learned thereafter that despair is but the hidden side of hope.'

"Here follow pages of his wanderings in quest of God. He tells how and where he inquired and sought, searching into the near and minute as earnestly as into the far and vast, watching at the very pores of being, and sitting in the gates of the mighty halls of assembly—but all in vain. No God was to be found.

"'And it seemed to me,' he says at last, 'that, as I had been the wanderer of earth, so was I now doomed to be the wanderer of heaven. On earth I wandered to find death, and men called me the everlasting Jew; in heaven I wandered to find God, and what name would they give me now?

"'At last my heart sank within me wholly, and I folded my wings, and through years I also sank and sank, and alighted at length upon the place appointed for my habitation—that namely wherein I found myself first after death. And alighting there, I fell down weary and slept.

"'And when I awoke I turned upon my side in the despair of a life that was neither in my own power nor in that of one who was the Father of me, which life therefore was an evil thing and a tyrant unto me. And lo! there by my side I beheld a lily of the field such as grew on the wayside in the old times betwixt Jerusalem and Bethany. Never since my death had I seen such, and my heart awoke within me, and I wept bitter tears that nothing should be true, nothing be that which it had seemed in the times of old. And as I wept I heard a sound as of the falling of many tears, and I looked, and lo a shower as from a watering-pot falling upon the lily! And I looked yet again, and I saw the watering-pot, and the hand that held it; and he whose hand held the pot stood by me and looked at me as he watered the lily. He was a man like the men of the world where such lilies grow, and was poorly dressed, and seemed like a gardener. And I looked up in his face, and lo—the eyes of the Lord Jesus! and my heart swelled until it filled my whole body and my head, and I gave a great cry, and for joy that turned into agony I could not rise, neither could I speak, but I crept on my hands and my knees to his feet, and there I fell down upon my face, and with my hands I lifted one of his feet and did place it upon my head, and then I found voice to cry, O master! and therewith the life departed from me. And when I came to myself the master sat under the tree, and I lay by his side, and he had lifted my head upon his knees. And behold, the world was jubilant around me, for Love was Love and Lord of all. The sea roared, and the fulness thereof was love; and the purple and the gold and the blue and the green came straight from the hidden red heart of the Lord Jesus. And I closed my eyes for very bliss; nor had I yet bethought me of the time when first those eyes looked upon me, for I seemed to have known them since first I began to be. But now when for very bliss I closed my eyes, my sin came back to me, and I remembered. And I rose up, and kneeled down before him, and said, O Lord, I am Ahasuerus the Jew, the man who would not let thee rest thy cross upon the stone before my workshop, but drave thee from it.—Say no more of that, answered my Lord, for truly I have myself rested in thy heart, cross and all, until the thing thou diddest in thy ignorance is better than forgotten, for it is remembered in love. Only see thou also make right excuse for my brethren who, like thee then, know not now what they do. Come and I will bring thee to the woman who died for thee in the burning fire. And I said, O Lord, leave me not, for although I would now in my turn right gladly die for her, yet would I not look upon that woman again if the love of her would make me love thee one hair the less— thou knowest. And the Lord smiled upon me and said, Fear not, Ahasuerus; my love infolds and is the nest of all love. I fear not; fear thou not either. And I arose and followed him. And every tree and flower, yea every stone and cloud, with the whole earth and sea and air, were full of God, even the living God—so that now I could have died of pure content. And I followed my Lord.'"

The gate-keeper was silent, and so were they all. At length Rachel rose softly, wiping the tears from her eyes, and left the room. But she found no one in the closet. Helen was already hastening across the park, weeping as she went.

CHAPTER XXIX.

THE CURATE'S RESOLVE.

The next day was Sunday.

Twelve months had not yet elapsed since the small events with which my narrative opened. The change which had passed, not merely upon the opinions, but in the heart and mind and very being of the curate, had not then begun to appear even to himself, although its roots were not only deep in him but deep beyond him, even in the source of him; and now he was in a state of mind, a state of being, rather, of whose nature at that time he had not, and could not have had, the faintest fore-feeling, the most shadowy conception. It had been a season of great trouble, but the gain had been infinitely greater; for now were the bonds of the finite broken, he had burst the shell of the mortal, and was of those over whom the second death hath no power. The agony of the second birth was past, and he was a child again— only a child, he knew, but a child of the kingdom; and the world, and all that God cared about in it, was his, as no miser's gold could ever belong to its hoarder, while the created universe, yea and the uncreated also whence it sprang, lay open to him in the boundless free-giving of the original Thought. "All things are yours, and ye are Christ's, and Christ is God's:" he understood the words even as he who said them understood them, and as the wise of this world never will understand them until first they become fools that they may be wise.

At the same time a great sorrow threatened him from the no less mysterious region of his relations to humanity; but if that region and its most inexplicable cares were beyond the rule of the Life that dwelt in him, then was that Life no true God, and the whole thing was false; for he loved Helen with a love that was no invention or creation of his own, and if not his, then whose? Certainly not of one who, when it threatened to overwhelm him, was unable to uphold him under it! This thing also belonged to the God of his being. A poor God must he be for men or women who did not care about the awful things involved in the relation between them! Therefore even in his worst anxieties about Helen,—I do not mean in his worst seasons of despair at the thought of never gaining her love—he had never yet indeed consciously regarded the winning of her as a possibility—but at those times when he most plainly saw her the submissive disciple of George Bascombe, and the two seemed to his fancy to be straying away together "into a wide field, full of dark mountains;" when he saw her, so capable of the noblest, submitting her mind to the entrance of the poorest, meanest, shabbiest theories of life, and taking for her guide one who could lead her to no conscious well-being, or make provision for sustainment when the time of suffering and anxiety should come, or the time of health and strength be over when yet she must live on; when he saw her adopting a system of things whose influence would shrivel up instead of developing her faculties, crush her imagination with such a mountain-weight as was never piled above Titan, and dwarf the whole divine woman within her to the size and condition of an Aztec—even then was he able to reason with himself: "She belongs to God, not to me; and God loves her better than ever I could love her. If she should set out with her blind guide, it will be but a first day's journey she will go—through marshy places and dry sands, across the far breadth of which, lo! the blue mountains that shelter the high vales of sweetness and peace." And with this he not only tried to comfort himself, but succeeded—I do not say to contentment, but to quiet. Contentment, which, whatever its immediate shape, to be contentment at all, must be the will of God, lay beyond. Alas that men cannot believe there is such a thing as "that good and acceptable and perfect will of God!" To those that do believe it, it is the rejoicing of a conscious deliverance.

And now this Sunday, Wingfold entered the pulpit prepared at last to utter his resolve. Happily nothing had been done to introduce the confusing element of another will. The bishop had heard nothing of the matter, and if anything had reached the rector, he had not spoken. Not one of the congregation, not even Mrs. Ramshorn, had hinted to him that he ought to resign. It had been left altogether with himself. And now he would tell them the decision to which the thought he had taken had conducted him. I will give a portion of his sermon—enough to show us how he showed the congregation the state of his mind in reference to the grand question, and the position he took in relation to his hearers.

"It is time, my hearers," he said, "because it is now possible, to bring to a close that uncertainty with regard to the continuance of our relation to each other, which I was, in the spring-time of the year, compelled by mental circumstance to occasion. I then forced myself, for very dread of the honesty of an all-knowing God, to break through every convention of the church and the pulpit, and speak to you of my most private affairs. I told you that I was sure of not one of those things concerning which it is taken for granted that a clergyman must be satisfied; but that I would not at once yield my office, lest in that act I should seem to declare unbelief of many a thing which even then I desired to find true. In leaving me undisturbed either by complaint, expostulation, or proffered instruction, you, my hearers, have granted me the leisure of which I stood in need. Meantime I have endeavoured to show you the best I saw, while yet I dared not say I was sure of anything. I have thus kept you, those at least who cared to follow my path, acquainted with my mental history. And now I come to tell you the practical result at which I have arrived.

"But when I say that I will not forsake my curacy, still less my right and duty to teach whatever I seem to know, I must not therein convey the impression that I have attained that conviction and assurance the discovery of the absence of which was the cause of the whole uncertain proceeding. All I now say is, that in the story of Jesus I have beheld such grandeur—to me apparently altogether beyond the reach of human invention, such a radiation of divine loveliness and truth, such hope for man, soaring miles above every possible pitfall of Fate; and have at the same time, from the endeavour to obey the word recorded as his, experienced such a conscious enlargement of mental faculty, such a deepening of moral strength, such an enhancement of ideal, such an increase of faith, hope, and charity towards all men, that I now declare with the consent of my whole man—I cast in my lot with the servants of the Crucified; I am content even to share their delusion, if delusion it be, for it is the truth of the God of men to me; I will stand or fall with the story of my Lord; I will take my chance—I speak not in irreverence but in honesty—my chance of failure or success in regard to whatever may follow in this life or the life to come, if there be a life to come—on the words and will of the Lord Jesus Christ, whom if, impressed as I am with the truth of his nature, the absolute devotion of his life, and the essential might of his being, I yet obey not, I shall not only deserve to perish, but in that very refusal draw ruin upon my head. Before God I say it—I would rather be crucified with that man, so it might be as a disciple and not as a thief that creeps, intrudes, or climbs into the fold, than I would reign with him over such a kingdom of grandeur as would have satisfied the imagination and love-ambition of his mother. On such grounds as these I hope I am justified in declaring myself a disciple of the Son of Man, and in devoting my life and the renewed energy and enlarged, yea infinite hope which he has given me, to his brothers and sisters of my race, that if possible I may gain some to be partakers of the blessedness of my hope. Henceforth I am, not IN HOLY ORDERS, I reject the phrase, but UNDER holy orders, even the orders of Christ Jesus, which is the law of liberty, the law whose obedience alone can set a man free from in-burrowing slavery.

"And if any man yet say that, because of my lack of absolute assurance, I have no right to the sacred post,—Let him, I answer, who has been assailed by such doubts as mine, and from the citadel of his faith sees no more one lingering shadow of a foe—let him cast at me the first stone! Vain challenge! for such a one will never cast a stone at man or woman. But let not him whose belief is but the absence of doubt, who has never loved enough that which he thinks he believes to have felt a single fear lest it should not be true—let not that man, I say, cast at me pebble from the brook, or cloven rock from the mount of the law, for either will fall hurtless at my feet. Friends, I have for the last time spoken of myself in this place. Ye have borne with me in my trials, and I thank you. Those who have not only borne but suffered, and do now rejoice with me, I thank tenfold. I have done—

"Save for one word to the Christians of this congregation:

"The waves of infidelity are coming in with a strong wind and a flowing tide. Who is to blame? God it cannot be, and for unbelievers, they are as they were. It is the Christians who are to blame. I do not mean those who are called Christians, but those who call and count themselves Christians. I tell you, and I speak to each one of whom it is true, that you hold and present such a withered, starved, miserable, death's-head idea of Christianity; that you are yourselves such poverty-stricken believers, if believers you are at all; that the notion you present to the world as your ideal, is so commonplace, so false to the grand, gracious, mighty-hearted Jesus—that YOU are the cause why the truth hangs its head in patience, and rides not forth on the white horse, conquering and to conquer. You dull its lustre in the eyes of men; you deform its fair proportions; you represent not that which it is, but that which it is not, yet call yourselves by its name; you are not the salt of the earth, but a salt that has lost its savour, for ye seek all things else first, and to that seeking the kingdom of God and his righteousness shall never be added. Until you repent and believe afresh, believe in a nobler Christ, namely the Christ revealed by himself, and not the muffled form of something vaguely human and certainly not all divine, which the false interpretations of men have substituted for him, you will be, as, I repeat, you are, the main reason why faith is so scanty in the earth, and the enemy comes in like a flood. For the sake of the progress of the truth, and that into nobler minds than yours, it were better you joined the ranks of the enemy, and declared what I fear with many of you is the fact, that you believe not at all. But whether in some sense you believe or not, the fact remains, that, while you are not of those Christians who obey the word of the master, DOING the things he says to them, you are of those Christians, if you WILL be called by the name, to whom he will say, I never knew you: go forth into the outer darkness. Then at least will the church be rid of you, and the honest doubter will have room to breathe the divine air of the presence of Jesus.

"But oh what unspeakable bliss of heart and soul and mind and sense remains for him who like St. Paul is crucified with Christ, who lives no more from his own self, but is inspired and informed and possessed with the same faith towards the Father in which Jesus lived and wrought the will of the Father! If the words attributed to Jesus are indeed the words of him whom Jesus declared himself, then truly is the fate of mankind a glorious one,—and that, first and last, because men have a God supremely grand, all-perfect in God-head; for that is, and that alone can be, the absolute bliss of the created."

CHAPTER XXX.

HELEN AWAKE.

That Sunday-dinner was a very quiet meal. An old friend of Mrs. Ramshorn, a lady-ecclesiastic like herself, dined with them; what the two may have said to each other in secret conclave, I cannot tell, but not a word of remark upon Mr. Wingfold or his sermon was heard at table.

As she was leaving the room, Bascombe whispered Helen to put on something and come to him in the garden. Helen glanced at the window as if doubtful. It was cold, but the sun was shining; the weather had nothing to do with it; she had but taken a moment to think. She pressed her lips together—and consented. George saw she would rather not go, but he set it down to a sisterly unwillingness to enjoy herself when her brother could no longer behold the sun, and such mere sentiment must not be encouraged.

When the cypresses and box-trees had come betwixt them and the house, he offered his arm, but Helen preferred being free. She did not refuse to go into the summer-house with him; but she took her place on the opposite side of the little table. George however spied no hint of approaching doom.

"I am sorry to have to alter my opinion of that curate," he said as he seated himself. "There was so much in him that I took to promise well. But old habit, the necessities of existence, and the fear of society have been too much for him—as they will always be for most men. He has succumbed at last, and I am sorry! I did think he was going to turn out an honest man!"

"And you have come to the certain conclusion that he is not an honest man, George?"

"Assuredly."

"Why?"

"Because he goes on to teach what he confesses he is not sure about."

"He professes to be sure that it is better than anything he is sure about.— You teach me there is no God: are you absolutely certain there is not?"

"Yes; absolutely certain."

"On what grounds?"

"On grounds I have set forth to you twenty times, Helen, dear," answered George a little impatiently. "I am not inclined to talk about them now.—I can no more believe in a god than in a dragon."

"And yet a dragon was believable to the poets that made our old ballads; and now geology reveals that some-such creatures did at one time actually exist."

"Ah! you turn the tables on me there, Helen! I confess my parallel a false one."

"A truer one than you think, perhaps," said Helen. "That a thing should seem absurd to one man, or to a thousand men, will not make it absurd in its own nature; and men as good and as clever as you, George, have in all ages believed in a God. Only their notion of God may have been different from yours. Perhaps their notion was a believable one, while yours is not."

"By Jove, Helen! you've got on with your logic. I feel quite flattered! So far as I am aware you have had no tutor in that branch but myself! You'll soon be too much for your master, by Jove!"

Like the pied piper, Helen smiled a little smile. But she said seriously,

"Well, George, all I have to suggest is—What if, after all your inability to believe it, things should at last prove, even to your— satisfaction, shall I say?—that there IS a God?"

"Don't trouble yourself a bit about it, Helen," returned George, whose mind was full of something else, to introduce which he was anxiously, and heedlessly, clearing the way: "I am prepared to take my chance, and all I care about is whether you will take your chance with me. Helen, I love you with my whole soul."

"Oh! you have a soul, then, George? I thought you hadn't!"

"It IS a foolish form of speech, no doubt," returned Bascombe, a little disconcerted, as was natural. "—But to be serious, Helen, I do love you."

"How long will you love me if I tell you I don't love you?"

"Really, Helen, I don't see how to answer such a question. I don't understand you at all to-day! Have I offended you? I am very sorry if I have, but I am quite in the dark as to when or where or how."

"Tell me then," said Helen, heedless of his evident annoyance and discomfort, "how long will you love me if I love you in return?"

"For ever and ever."

"Another form of speech?"

"You know what I mean well enough. I shall love you as long as I live."

"George, I never could love a man who believed I was going to die for ever."

"But, Helen," pleaded Bascombe, "if it can't be helped, you know!"

"But you are content it should be so. You believe it willingly. You scoff at any hint of a possible immortality."

"Well, but, Helen, what difference can it make between you and ᵢ returned George, whom the danger of losing her had rendered for moment indifferent even to his most cherished theory. "If there shoulᵈ anything afterwards, of course I should go on loving you to the very extre of the possible."

"While now you don't love me enough to wish I may live and not die! Leaviᵢ that out of view however, it makes all the difference to the love I should havᵢ to expect of you. It may be only a whim—I can prove nothing any more thaᵢ you—but I have a—whim then—to be loved as an immortal woman, the child of a living God, and not as a helpless bastard of Nature!—I beg your pardon—I forget my manners."

That a lady should utter such a word!—and that lady, Helen!—George was shocked. Coming on the rest, it absolutely bewildered him. He sat silent perforce. Helen saw it, and yielded to a moment's annoyance with herself, but presently resumed:

"I have given you the advantage, George, and wronged myself. But I don't care MUCH. I shall only take the better courage to speak my mind.—You come asking me to love you, and my brother lying mouldering in the earth— all there is of him, you tell me! If you believed he was alive still, and I should find him again some day, there would be no reason why you should not speak of love even now; for where does anyone need love more than at the brink of the grave? But to come talking of love to me, with the same voice that has but just been teaching me that the grave is the end of all, and my brother gone down into it for ever—I tell you, cousin—I must say it—it seems to me hardly decent. For me at least—I will NOT be loved with the love that can calmly accept such a fate. And I will never love any man, believing that, if I outlive him, my love must thereafter be but a homeless torrent, falling ever into a bottomless abyss. Why should I make of my heart a roaring furnace of regrets and self-accusations? The memory of my brother is for me enough. Let me keep what freedom is possible to me; let me rather live the life of a cold-blooded animal, and die in the ice that gathers about me. But before I sit down to await such an end, I shall know whether I am indeed compelled to believe as you do that there is no God, that Death is my lord and master, that he will take me as he has taken my brother and yet I shall never see him more. No, cousin George, I need a God; and if there be none how did I come to need one? Yes, I know you think you can explain it all, but the way you account for it is just as miserable as what you would put in its place. I am not complete in myself like you. I am not able to live without a God. I will seek him until I find him, or drop into the abyss where all question and answer ceases. Then in the end I shall be no worse than you would have me at the beginning—no, it will be nothing so bad, for then I shall not know my misery as you would have me know it now. If we are

ne?"
the
be
ne

g

spite of all the outcry of our souls against that fate,
it if, thus utterly befooled of Nature, we should also a
by believing in a lovely hope that looks like a promise,
ight to be true? How can a devotion to the facts of her
ed of one whose nature has been proved to her a lie?—
he facts of your nature, George; I speak from the facts of

e awake at last! It would have suited George better had she
lf-quickened statue, responsive only to himself, her not over-
alion. He sat speechless—with his eyes fixed on her.

no God," she went on, "therefore you seek none. If you need
are right to seek none, I dare say. But I need a God—oh, I cannot
I need him, if he be to be found! and by the same reasoning I will
life to the search for him. To the last I will go on seeking him, for if
give in, and confess there is no God, I shall go mad—mad, and
ps kill somebody like poor Poldie. George, I have said my say. I would
iave come into the garden but to say it. Good-bye."

she spoke she rose and held out her hand to him. But in the tumult of
ore emotions than I can well name—amongst the rest indignation, dismay,
isappointment, pride, and chagrin, he lost himself while searching in vain
for words, paid no heed to her movement, and lifted no hand to take that
she offered.

With head erect she walked from the summer-house.

"The love of a lifetime!—a sweet invitation!" she said to herself, as with the
slow step of restrained wrath she went up the garden.

George sat for some minutes as she had left him. Then he broke the silence
in his own ears and said,

"Well, I'm damned!"

And so he was—for the time—and a very good thing too, for he required it.

CHAPTER XXXI.

THOU DIDST NOT LEAVE.

The next day the curate found himself so ill at ease, from the reaction after excitement of various kinds, that he determined to give himself a holiday. His notion of a holiday was a very simple one: a day in a deep wood, if such could be had, with a volume fit for alternate reading and pocketing as he might feel inclined. Of late no volume had been his companion in any wanderings but his New Testament.

There was a remnant of real old-fashioned forest on the Lythe, some distance up: thither he went by the road, the shortest way, to return by the winding course of the stream. It was a beautiful day of St. Martin's summer. In the forest, if the leaves were gone, there was the more light, and sun and shadow played many a lovely game. But he saw them as though he saw them not, for fear and hope struggled in his heart, and for a long time prayer itself could not atone them. At length a calm fell, and he set out to return home, down the bank of the river.

Many-hued and many-shaped had been the thoughts, not that came to him from the forest, but that he had carried thither with him: through all and each of them, ever and again had come dawning the face of Helen, as he had seen it in church the day before, where she sat between her aunt and her cousin, so unlike either. For, to their annoyance, she had insisted on going to church, and to hers, they had refused to let her go alone. And in her face the curate had seen something he had never seen there until then,—a wistful look, as if now she would be glad to pick up any suitable crumb to carry home with her. In that dawn of coming childhood, though he dared not yet altogether believe it such, the hard contemptuous expression of Bascombe's countenance, and the severe disapproval in Mrs. Ramshorn's, were entirely lost upon him.

All the way down the river, the sweet change haunted him. When he got into the park, and reached that hollow betwixt the steep ferny slopes where he sat on the day with which my narrative opens, he seated himself again on the same stone, and reviewed the past twelve months. This was much such a day as that, only the hour was different: it was the setting sun that now shone upon the ferns, and cast shadows from them big enough for oaks. What a change had passed upon him! That day the New Testament had been the book of the church—this day it was a fountain of living waters to the man Thomas Wingfold. He had not opened his Horace for six months. Great trouble he had had; both that and its results were precious. Now a new trouble had come, but that also was a form of life: he would rather love and suffer and love still, a thousand times rather, than return to the poverty of not knowing Helen Lingard; yet a thousand times rather would he forget

Helen Lingard than lose from his heart one word of the Master, whose love was the root and only pledge and security of love, the only power that could glorify it—could cleanse it from the mingled selfishness that wrought for its final decay and death.

The sun was down ere he left the park, and the twilight was rapidly following the sun as he drew near to the Abbey on his way home. Suddenly, more like an odour than a sound, he heard the organ, he thought. Never yet had he heard it on a week-day: the organist was not of those who haunt their instrument. Often of late had the curate gazed on that organ as upon a rock filled with sweet waters, before which he stood a Moses without his rod; sometimes the solemn instrument appeared to him a dumb Jeremiah that sat there from Sunday to Sunday, all the week long, with his head bowed upon his hands, and not a Jebusite to listen to him: if only his fingers had been taught the craft, he thought, how his soul would pour itself out through the song-tubes of that tabernacle of sweetness and prayer, and on the blast of its utterance ascend to the throne of the most high! Who could it be that was now peopling the silence of the vast church with melodious sounds, worshipping creatures of the elements? If the winds and the flames of fire are his augels, how much more the grandly consorting tones of the heavenly organ! He would go and see what power informed the vaporous music.

He entered the church by one of the towers, in which a stair led skyward, passing the neighbourhood of the organ, and having a door to its loft. As he ascended, came a pause in the music;—and then, like the breaking up of a summer cloud in the heavenliest of rain-showers, began the prelude to the solo in the Messiah, THOU DIDST NOT LEAVE HIS SOUL IN HELL. Up still the curate crept softly. All at once a rich full contralto voice—surely he had heard it before—came floating out on the torrent, every tone bearing a word of sorrowful triumph in its bosom.

He reached the door. Very gently he opened it, and peeped in. But the back of the organ was towards him, and he could see nothing. He stepped upon the tiles of the little apse. One stride cleared the end of the organ, and he saw the face of the singer: it WAS Helen Lingard!

She started. The music folded its wings and dropped—like a lark into its nest. But Helen recovered herself at once, rose from her ministration at the music-altar, and approached the curate.

"Have I taken too great a liberty?" she said, in a gentle, steady voice.

"No, surely," he answered. "I am sorry I startled you. I wish you would wake such sounds oftener."

"He didn't leave my brother's soul in hell, did he, Mr. Wingfold?" she said abruptly, and her eyes shone through the dusk.

"If ever a soul was taken out of hell, it was Leopold's," returned the curate. "And it lifts mine out of it too," he added, "to hear you say so."

"I behaved very badly to you. I confess my fault. Will you forgive me?" she said.

"I love you too much to be able to forgive you:" that was the word in the curate's heart, but a different found its way to his lips.

"My heart is open to you, Miss Lingard," he said: "take what forgiveness you think you need. For what I can tell, it may be my part to ask forgiveness, not to grant it. If I have been harder to you than there was need, I pray you to forgive me. Perhaps I did not enter enough into your difficulties."

"You never said one word more than was right, or harder than I deserved. Alas! I can no more—in this world at least—ask Leopold to forgive me, but I can ask you and Mr. Polwarth, who were as the angels of God to him, to pardon me for him and for yourselves too. I was obstinate and proud and selfish.—Oh, Mr. Wingfold, can you, do you really believe that Leopold is somewhere? Is he alive this moment? Shall I ever—ever—I don't mind if it's a thousand years first—but shall I EVER see him again?"

"I do think so. I think the story must be true that tells us Jesus took to himself again the body he left on the cross, and brought it with him out of its grave."

"Will you take me for a pupil—a disciple—and teach me to believe—or hope, if you like that word better—as you do?" said Helen humbly.

How the heart of the curate beat—like the drum of a praising orchestra!

"Dear Miss Lingard," he answered, very solemnly, "I can teach you nothing; I can but show you where I found what has changed my life from a bleak November to a sunny June—with its thunder-storms no doubt—but still June beside November. Perhaps I could help you a little if you were really set out to find Jesus, but you must yourself set out. It is you who must find him. Words of mine, as the voice of one crying in the wilderness, may let you know that one is near who thinks he sees him, but it is you who must search, and you who must find. If you do search, you will find, with or without help of mine.—But it is getting dark.—You have the key of the north door, I suppose?"

"Yes."

"Then will you lock the door, and take the key to Mrs. Jenkins. I will stay here a while, and then follow you home, if you will allow we, where we can have a little talk together. Ah, what an anthem the silent organ will play for me!"

Helen turned and went down into the church, and thence home.

The curate remained with the organ. It was silent, and so were his lips, but his heart—the music was not latent there, for his praise and thanksgiving ascended, without voice or instrument, essential harmony, to the ear that hears thought, and the heart that vibrates to every chord of feeling in the hearts it has created. Ah! what is it we send up thither, where our thoughts are either a dissonance or a sweetness and a grace? Alone in the dusky church, the curate's ascended like a song of the angels, for his heart was all a thanksgiving—not for any perfected gift, but for many a lovely hope. He knelt down by the organ and worshipped the God and Father of the Lord Jesus Christ—that God and no other was the God of his expectation. When he rose from his knees, the church was dark, but through the windows of the clerestory many stars were shining.

THE END.

Milton Keynes UK
Ingram Content Group UK Ltd.
UKHW010842110324
438959UK00019B/346